Micha Max, Lloyd and Jake

by John Warren

Michael, Max, Lloyd and Jake (First Edition)

Published by John Warren & Amazon Publishing

Published 2021.
First edition published 2021.
Printed in the United Kingdom.

ISBN 9798777733993

Contents

Chapter One	Michael	Page 5
Chapter Two	Danielle	Page 17
Chapter Three	Max	Page 29
Chapter Four	Hirioto Onyo	Page 37
Chapter Five	Lloyd	Page 47
Chapter Six	Ernesto Pontes	Page 55
Chapter Seven	Jake	Page 65
Chapter Eight	Poppy	Page 73
Chapter Nine	Mrs Pilot	Page 85
Chapter Ten	Joanna	Page 99
Chapter Eleven	Mrs Browning	Page 109
Chapter Twelve	Judge Adams	Page 121
Chapter Thirteen	Mr Starr	Page 131
Chapter Fourteen	Miriam	Page 145
Chapter Fifteen	Elz	Page 157
Chapter Sixteen	Tim Harrop	Page 173
Chapter Seventeen	The Three Ministers	Page 189
Chapter Eighteen	Phil	Page 197
Chapter Nineteen	Lloyd's Father	Page 207
Chapter Twenty	Francois	Page 213
Chapter Twenty One	Prime Minister King	Page 219

Chapter One

Michael

The four boys walked up the hallway to the head teacher's office in total silence. They couldn't help but each glance at Poppy as they walked past. She was sitting by herself in a chair outside the office. She looked up at each of them.

Her shoulders were hunched, and her toes pointed together. They saw fear, they saw danger and they saw a hint of defiance in her eyes.

But she would have her own battle. Right now they were concerned about what was going to happen to them. They entered the office. It was one of the few parts of the school they didn't recognise.

They were unsure where to stand. The office was big, the desk was big, and their hearts were beating fast. And their head teacher looked hostile. In a split second they all knew that she didn't like them, and she didn't care that they knew it.

"Right!" the head teacher, Mrs. Pilot, said loudly, as she looked carefully at the four boys in front of her. Her voice was angry.

She sized each of them up. In her head they were not good students or bad students - that's not how she thought. They were simply easy to control or difficult to control. Those were the categories that mattered to her. Michael was the one who was the leader, if Jake could be brought to heel. Michael would lead but he generally had no habit of leading people into trouble. Good. Max and Lloyd would likely follow Michael's lead. Jake was a complete wildcard and didn't care to follow anyone. She disliked Jake greatly. She spoke to them in a voice more suited to a room three times as large as the one they were in:

"You four boys listen closely to me. The four of you are each going to sit down and write out for me exactly what happened. I don't care how long it takes. I don't care what class you have next. I don't care how much paper you need. You will spend the next hour - the next two hours - the next however long it takes - and you are going to tell me everything that occurred. I want to know what she did, what she said and what you saw. You are not going to leave any details out. You are not going to rush. And you are definitely, certainly not going to lie."

She leaned forward. She glared at them. She paused for effect.

"Is that clear?"

"Yes, Mrs Pilot" the four boys each muttered in reply.

She was going for a high level of intimidation. She had worked hard to reach her position as head teacher. There was no way she was going to let an unexpected incident cause her grip to loosen. She was not particularly old for a head teacher, but she dressed as if she was. An appearance of age added to her authority. What the students didn't realise (and didn't care about) was that half of Mrs Pilot's time was spent trying to control the staff. They were just as much a problem as the students were. And it is always easier to assert authority over someone younger than you. So the older you appeared to be, the easier life as a head teacher was. This is what Mrs Pilot had intuitively worked out. She made no attempt to colour or hide her grey hairs. Her hair was cut short and perfectly styled to look as professional as possible. Actually it would be more accurate to called it "organised" rather than "styled." She maintained a high energy level and was always across anything that might be a problem. Appear professional and put out fires quickly - this was her approach to the job, and she stayed at the top of the tree because of it.

She had grown up as the eldest child of five, and knew a great deal about the need for control.

She naturally followed her mother's systems and rules, and showed leadership when her parents were not around. None of her siblings ever asked for her leadership, but they got it regardless. What they wanted didn't really come into it. She had always had ambition. She had little time for those who lacked it.

She had even less time for those with ambition that would threaten hers. And right now her control was being tested by four boys, one girl, one ambulance in the school driveway and two distressed parents.

For Michael, Max, Lloyd and Jake some writing paper was found. The boys were worried.

They knew it was serious, even though they were not the ones accused. With paper in hand they made their way out of the head teacher's office. One of the administration staff told each of them where to go.

Every single one of them stole a quick glance at Poppy as they came out the door. Poppy sat on the same chair outside the office. She was crying. She glanced up at them, just as she did when they entered a few minutes ago. She didn't look like a criminal. In fact it seemed that nothing criminal had happened. But she was in so much trouble.

Michael was given a desk in the administration office. The staff there knew what had happened. The administration office was just near the driveway, and the ambulance was still sitting there. Eleazar's parents were standing outside it, and Eleazar was sitting in a wheelchair. Michael could hear raised voices, people shouting. He put it out of his mind, and tried to concentrate. His head and heart were racing granted what had happened just 20 minutes ago. He glanced around looking for a pen. There was one a few metres away on another desk. No one was using it, so he looked at it closely for two seconds. It moved through the air, across the room and right into his hand.

He had to get his account correct. He decided to be truthful. He would give too much detail rather than not enough. He began to write:

Poppy was born on the same day as me. We grew up around the corner. I live on School Lane, and her family lives on Woodland Terrace. We knew her family a bit because of the birthday thing. We didn't play much because she's a girl and I play football with the boys. I knew her at primary school. We have always been at the same school. I know that she's smart. She's always been smart. She was at the top table for maths all through primary school, same as me. She reads books, and gets good scores in her exams.

A few weeks ago Mrs Anderson gave us a group work task. Poppy and I were not happy because we knew that we would end up carrying the group. Poppy complained that she was the only girl in the group. The others don't care about their schoolwork much. The group was Poppy, me, Max, Lloyd, Jake and Elz. Obviously Elz (Eleazar, I mean) was not there much because of his illness. We had to do a presentation to the history class about the Black Death.

Michael started to get into the flow of his writing. He didn't mind this task as he found that it was a good way of getting straight in his head what had just happened.

Michael was generally unaware that he was a leader. He was aware that he got good marks. But that was unrelated to his personality. He figured he was nothing special because he was average height, average build, with brown hair and brown eyes. He was incapable of physically standing out in a crowd, unless he travelled to another continent or something.

But he looked people in the eye, his back was

straight, he projected confidence and he spoke with a strong voice. Michael didn't realise that he did these things and that most people did not.

He didn't realise that people are naturally drawn to those qualities. And for those reasons people followed him, even though he wasn't trying to lead them.

Michael had never really had anything major go wrong in his life. When he dropped a piece of bread it generally landed with the buttered side up.

He wasn't arrogant, but he was confident. He smiled quickly and found that the things people asked of him were simple to achieve. He couldn't remember ever being in the head teacher's office before. But he wasn't too worried because he knew he had done nothing wrong. No one had.

He continued writing:

Mrs Anderson got us to break off into the four groups who were presenting on different things. Our group was sent to room 29 because it wasn't being used that lesson. This was the third time we had been planning it, and there would only be one more before we had to do it in front of the class. Poppy had pushed Elz's wheelchair from the room we were in at the start to room 29. When we sat down we were near the window because the sun was coming in. It was nice. We talked about the presentation for a couple of minutes. Lloyd wanted to be a dead body and Max wanted to use lots of special effects make up. To be honest no one cared very much - we hadn't made much progress and I think it was going to be left to the last minute.

As the lesson went on we stopped talking about it and talked amongst ourselves. Max pulled out his phone and he and Lloyd started watching football highlights. Jake and I both got our maths homework out and were getting it done, and asking each other when we had something we didn't know. Elz was tired. He was sitting across the table from me. I don't know why he comes in to school when he is this unwell. He put his head down on the table and fell asleep. With the sun coming through the windows directly onto us I thought I might soon do the same.

Poppy was sat at the head of the table, with Elz on her right and me on her left. Once we stopped talking about the history task she looked like she might be sleeping as well. She had her eyes closed but her head stayed upright. She reached out her right hand and rested it gently on Elz's arm, not that he would have known.

Poppy and Elz have always been close. But there's never been anything romantic between them. They don't hang out with the same group of friends, they don't have many classes together or anything, but they have always got on well. She took it real hard when he first got sick. There's nothing she can do - the doctors are in charge of his treatment and his family are close and support him. She's not needed. But I know she cares for him. She was happy that he came to school today, and that he is in our group.

Michael paused. The hard part was about to begin. He had to put into ordinary words some very extraordinary things. Michael closed his eyes for a moment and went through his memories of what had just happened. It was crazy. He shook his head without realising that he was doing it. He picked up his pen and kept writing:

> *Then things got strange. At some point I looked at Poppy and she had a funny look on her face. Her eyes were closed, but she was concentrating hard. Then I looked down her arm and saw that the hand she had on Elz's arm was now holding on really tight around his upper arm. It was his left arm because he was resting his head on his lower arm and facing away from Poppy as he slept.*

> *I said to Poppy, "Hey that's too tight. What are you doing?"*

> *Poppy didn't say anything back to me. She looked like she was in a trance or something. Then she started talking. She started talking softly under her breath. I don't know what she was saying. She was talking fast. Then it changed. She said something like, "This is what is right. This is the moment for what is good." But it was a strange voice. I had never heard her voice like that. She was in charge - she spoke like it was a command, but I have never heard Poppy talk like that. Actually I have never heard anyone talk anything like that. I'm not sure I know who*

was talking. I mean, Poppy was talking, but it didn't sound like Poppy.

Elz then jerked his head up off the table. I didn't know he was even capable of moving that fast anymore. Poppy was holding onto his arm tighter than ever, really tight. It should have been hurting but he didn't seem to notice. Then Poppy screamed at the top of her voice, "Now!" and she slammed her left fist down on the table. She let go of Elz with her right hand and slumped back into her chair. It's like she was dazed by what had happened.

But just then Elz stood up. None of us were expecting him to do that. He can only take a few steps, usually to get from the wheelchair into the car. Because he was sitting across from me I was looking right at him. And then he opened his eyes and stared at me. His eyes looked like they were dancing. It was like I could see deep inside him and he was alive, he was filled with energy, with fire. I know this sounds strange but I'm meant to give every detail and this is the detail that I remember stronger than any other. I expect I'll remember those eyes long after I've forgotten every other detail about this.

All of us were still, and were looking up at Elz. Then his glance came down and he looked straight at me. He was standing there, looking at me, and he began to smile. His lips slowly went up at the edges and he ended up with a huge grin on his face. His whole face looked so alive I couldn't believe it. I haven't seen him look that good since he first got - well actually, I have never seen him look so good.

He kept smiling but raised his hands above his head and then shouted, "Yes!" It was really loud, like when your team scores in a football match.

Then everyone started moving. Max flew out of the room to get someone. I wasn't looking at Poppy but a few seconds later she and Elz gave each other a big hug. Poppy started crying. I jumped up to see if Elz needed help getting back into his wheelchair, or to make sure he didn't fall and hurt himself. Lloyd and Jake did the same thing.

Elz was talking loudly. I don't know what he was saying. Everyone was talking at once. Poppy was talking, and the three of us who were still seeing how Elz was were all talking to him and trying to work out what had happened. Elz was smiling and I think he was saying that he felt full of life.

Suddenly Mrs Greening came into the room, with Max right behind her. She asked, "What's going on?" She saw that Elz was standing up and asked him if he was OK. He said he was great. His voice was loud and confident. I haven't heard him talk like that for months. I think Mrs Greening thought he was delusional, because he was still smiling. She told him to sit back in his wheelchair.

Within a few more minutes Elz was wheeled out of the room, and Mrs Greening told us to stay. The ambulance was called. We didn't really know what had happened or what we should do next. I still don't know.

Michael finished writing. It had taken him an hour and a half to write that account but he was no less shaken by the end than when he started. He had never seen anything like what had just happened.

Writing it down made him realise just how bizarre the whole thing was. But he knew that what had happened needed to be told. Deep down he was pleased that he could put it in writing while it was still fresh in his mind. He stopped and closed his eyes for a second. He was drawn to think about the lights that were dancing in Elz's eyes. He remembered them again. They were like magic, like fire, like beauty and like the stars all at once.

He told one of the administration staff that he was finished. He handed his letter to them, and was told to go back to class. There were only a few minutes until school was finished for the day, but he had a feeling that the day's drama was not yet complete. Normally life gets a lot more relaxed after the final bell. But there was nothing normal about today at all.

Chapter Two

Danielle

Telekinesis (tel-ee-kin-ee-sis) - the ability to move, manipulate or influence objects with the mind.

D anielle Tunupingu is sometimes described as an overnight sensation. In reality it was much quicker than that. Ten years ago she was a 16 year old, and was one day at home with her three younger brothers. It was a Wednesday morning during the school holidays. She lived in a remote part of Australia, where her tribe and ancestors had always lived. One of her younger brothers was filming her on his new phone, so she decided to do some tricks for him.

She made an apple move towards the camera, and then turn around in mid air, and go back to the table where it had been resting. When the dog walked through the room it started walking through the air.

Her brothers laughed at the dog's confusion at what was happening.

Danielle didn't find it freaky or strange - there had always been stories handed down in her tribe of people doing things like that. She believed the stories. She had done things like this before. It was no big deal. In her mind there was no sharp divide between the ordinary and the magical. She didn't know of a boundary between the regular and the miraculous. She just knew that she had been handed down stories about the country where she lived and her people's place in it.

Her brother uploaded the video onto the internet. His friends saw it straight away. They loved it. They shared it. Then others saw it. They loved it too. They shared it. And so on, and on, and on.

Millions saw it within the first thirty minutes. There are no borders online, so people in numerous countries were now watching Danielle's apple and her dog doing things that apples and dogs normally don't do. And they kept on sharing, because the video was so intriguing. What had been uploaded was so amazing and so compelling that only two conclusions were possible: either Danielle had the power to move objects with her mind, or she and her brothers were highly-skilled makers of fake videos. But it just didn't look fake at all.

Within an hour of the video being uploaded at 9am local time, news organisations started to notice. An amusing viral video makes for entertaining TV.

If the maker is local then there's a decent human interest story there to fill a short slot on the nightly news.

The city of Brisbane was a three hour drive from where Danielle lived. In Channel Seven's studios a TV news editor scratched around for a good story. He saw the video and when he learnt that Danielle lived not too far away he decided that an interview with Danielle would do the trick.

But who would he send? On his team of reporters no one wanted it.

Three hours there, and three hours back, just to interview someone for making a decent video online? Everyone quickly chose to look busy with other stories. So the job ended up with the most junior reporter on the team.

Sally Georgiou headed out to Danielle's tiny little town. She was about to break the biggest news story for centuries, but she was completely unaware of this. Her mood was foul. This time next week Sally would be famous, and her role in bringing Danielle to the world's attention would go down in history. But right in that moment Sally was grumpy.

Sally was joined by a cameraman, Rick Burns. Rick didn't know what to make of how his day had turned out. He would spend almost all of it in the car with Sally. Sally was pretty, which was good, but Sally was a snob, which was bad. Talking to Sally for six minutes would be a challenge for him. Six hours would be impossible. As it was the radio would be his saviour.

Three hours later Sally and Rick arrived at Danielle's house. Sally had found the drive painfully long. The only thing that made it bearable was that she and Rick had similar tastes in music. Arriving in the lousy little town Sally watched over the video once more on her phone. It really was clever - she could see why it had gained such a huge response.

All she had to do now was film a few words with Danielle for the camera, smile, say something catchy and then she would be on her (air-conditioned) way back to Brisbane. And Danielle would surely oblige - everyone loved to have their few minutes of fame on the nightly news.

Sally loved being on TV. She had been doing it for the last three years. There was no point at which the novelty had worn off. She loved being recognised when she went out in public. She went out a lot. Whilst Sally was only in her late 20's she was totally delighted with how her life had turned out.

She knew that she looked good. She was becoming a public figure. She got well paid for what she did. When she thought about all the losers that she had gone to High School with, she just wanted to shove her success in their faces. She was going places, and she had only just started. As she got out of the car and she looked around where Danielle lived. It wasn't nice, and she didn't want to be there for a minute longer than she had to be. But she knew that in a few minutes they would have filmed some footage, and tonight she would be back in the big city doing something fun.

Danielle and her family couldn't quite believe that she was there.

"What show you from?" Danielle asked.

"Channel Seven News in Brisbane." Sally replied.

"True?"

"Yes, I am."

"You're not.   You're having a lend."   Her brothers laughed at the thought of it.

"Well Danielle I certainly am, and I'd like to interview you about the video. Everyone's talking about it."

"Call me Danni."

Ten minutes later Rick's camera and Sally were in place. Three of those minutes were spent mastering the pronunciation of Danielle's surname. The other seven were spent trying to make Sally look perfect despite the heat and humidity. When they were all set Rick delivered the line they paid him for - "Camera rolling in five, four, three, two, one..."

"Sally Georgiou here with Danni Tunupingu, who has turned the internet upside down today with the video of her moving things with her mind. So Danni, is the video real, or a clever bit of trickery?"

"Ah yeah, it's real. No tricks in it."

"Really? Wow! Haha! Do you think you could move some things around for us now?"

Because Danni knew that it was real, and because she had known stories of it happening her whole life, Danni forgot that other people would think it was fake. Danni quickly saw from Sally's reaction that this reporter thought she was a fraud. She had come all this way just to make fun of her!

So if the rude lady wanted something to move, Danni decided to oblige. As Sally stood there with perfectly made up face and crazy perfect, bright, white teeth, Danni looked at the microphone Sally was holding in her hand. Two seconds later the microphone broke free from Sally's grip, flew up and bumped Sally flush on the nose. Her head went backwards and she was thrown off balance.

"Cut" yelled Rick.

"What the hell was that?" asked Sally.

Danni's brothers were laughing.

"You wanted something to move. So it did."

"Ow. That hurt!" As Sally regained her balance and worked out that it was just a little bump, her mind processed what Danni had just said. "What - are you telling me you made that microphone move out of my hand?"

"Musn't a been cos it's all tricks I thought you said."

Sally stared, not knowing what to say. Surely this young girl couldn't be for real. And yet she had felt the microphone move in her hand. The video was compelling. Perhaps there was more to the story than she thought. Her mind raced. Her mouth hung open but no sounds were coming out. But strangely, at that moment something unusual happened. Out of nowhere Sally had a moment of inspiration. She came across a nugget of wisdom, and changed her entire approach to the interview. She opened her mouth and out fell the best two sentences of Sally's whole life. She said, "Sorry Danni, I think I've approached this the wrong way. Why don't we sit down and you tell me your story?"

An hour later Sally was a believer. Whilst listening she had seen almost every object in the room move through the air. She had heard of Danni's ancestors, of their stories, of her life in this remote part of Australia, of her family, of her tribe and what they value. And at this point Danni dropped the key - the piece of information that would change everything.

"I can only do it when I've had nuts."

"Huh? Which nuts?"

"These ones." Danni pointed. "You call them macadamia nuts."

"What do the nuts do?"

"It's part of the story. Can't happen without them."

Sally was beginning to think that she was in the presence of a freak of nature - that Danni was some giant step forward in human development. But perhaps that was not the case. Perhaps...

"Do you think anyone could move things like you if they ate some nuts?"

"Sure."

Sally didn't know what to say. Her mind was moving a thousand miles an hour. "So... do you think ... I could?"

"Sure. Nothing special about me."

Sally's hands started trembling as she ate a macadamia from the bowl on the table.

"You need more." Danni said, "But there are trees all around here. Always has been."

"Hey!" Danni shouted to her little brothers. "Get the lady some more nuts."

Ten minutes later and with a dozen empty macadamia shells lying next to her Sally put the microphone on the floor in front of where she was sitting. She focussed her mind on the microphone. The boys were cheering her on. She looked intently at it. She willed it to move - her mind told it to rise from where it lay.

It moved.

Sally screamed. Rick jumped into the air as if the microphone was a giant spider. The microphone clattered back to the ground, having risen about 30 centimetres into the air. Danni and the boys roared with laughter at their reactions.

Sally screamed, "Oh my God! Did you see that? Oh! Oh! I don't believe it." She staggered around the room - she couldn't keep still. Her head felt like it might explode. Her hand shook like a leaf in the wind as she pointed to the microphone. "Did you see that? Did you see that?"

Rick couldn't believe how this afternoon was turning out. He figured his day would be a whole lot of driving - instead he had seen things he never imagined possible. He wondered if he was dreaming. He looked like he had seen a ghost - in fact a ghost would have been a welcome relief granted what was going on around him. But he knew what he had to do next. He thrust his hand into the pile of macadamia nuts and started eating.

As Rick began to chew it was now 2:30pm on Australia's east coast. And from here events unfolded quickly.

At 3pm Danni's brother posted another video of Sally and Rick moving objects around the room. Both of them were giddy with excitement. They had more energy than children on Christmas morning. This one was viewed even more than the first. But crucially the two minute video included Sally saying that the macadamia nuts were the thing that enabled her to do it. Internet search engines started to notice that searches for "macadamia nuts" were rising.

By 3:30pm supermarkets around Australia noticed significant numbers of people coming in to buy macadamia nuts and nothing else.

By 4pm seven more videos had been uploaded by people around Australia, one in Malaysia and one in New Zealand - people who were terrified, shaking and all testifying that they were moving objects around with nothing more than their thoughts after eating macadamias.

By 4:30pm the trickle of macadamia nut customers had turned into a flood. Every supply in Australia and many Asian nations were drained that very afternoon. Videos poured onto the internet from Vietnam, China, Japan, South Korea and Thailand.

They were being uploaded in such quantity that they began to dominate the global online conversation. Social media was followed by traditional media who saw that there was some sort of global frenzy around this story. Experts were trotted out to talk about madness and hysteria. Other experts were trotted out to explain why you can't make things move with your mind. However people were not mad, they were not in the grasp of some mania - but they certainly were moving things with their minds.

In America some night owls on the West Coast who had yet to go to bed caught the news.

Throughout Los Angeles, San Francisco and Seattle people poured into every 24 hour supermarket they could find, shopping for macadamias. Such was the screaming and shouting that followed every time someone gave it a try that half of California was awake just an hour or two after they had gone to bed.

At this time people in Africa and in Europe were waking up and checking their social media accounts. All anyone was talking about was making objects move with your thoughts and about macadamia nuts. When shops opened across Europe and Africa there were queues of people who had only one thing on their mind. There was not a single macadamia left on the shelf of a single European or African shop ten minutes after they opened for the day. And just minutes later, once the shock and surprise had been overcome, the videos flooded onto the internet.

The world was in uproar. Presidents and Prime Ministers all over the planet started to be briefed about what was going on. Most were instantly sceptical. Except for the ones that gave it a try. They knew that it was for real. Scientists fumbled for explanations, business people fumbled for how to profit from it, and historians fumbled for its significance. No one could believe that it was possible. Yet it was, as Danielle had always known.

Meanwhile back in Australia it was now evening. And the most famous Australian in the world was Danielle Tunupingu. She was more of a "same day sensation" than an overnight one.

—

In English the proper word for the ability to move things with your mind is "telekinesis." Which, at five syllables, was way too long a word to be used heavily without getting shortened. Someone, somewhere shortened it to 'teek' and it stuck. Over the next few weeks the word 'teek' became the most common word used to describe the new phenomenon. It was mostly used as a verb - "He teeked it over there." There were teeking competitions, and people would practice their 'teek skills.'

Also coming in at a very problematic five syllables was the word macadamia. This was sometimes shortened to "mac." Often it was not used at all - when you said "nuts" everyone knew that you were not talking about peanuts or cashews.

In the days following the discovery of teeking the world's entire supply of macadamia nuts was consumed. The demand for more was massive.

Wave after wave of trees were planted all around the world. Seven years later the new trees were dropping significant quantities of nuts, and with more coming into maturity every year the global market reached some kind of balance. It was just thousands of times bigger than what it had been before. The result was that most people around the world now had access to shops selling macadamias, and they could afford to buy enough to have ten each morning. This was all that you needed to be able to teek all day. And since teeking was the most fun thing in the world, pretty much everyone - man, woman and child - had their ten nuts each morning, and went around teeking throughout their day.

Chapter Three

Max

Max was told to find somewhere to sit and write in the woodwork room, which was not being used that afternoon. He fearfully walked through the corridors and then into the empty classroom. It felt strange to have the whole room to himself. He didn't want to be there. He found a desk close to the door. That way as soon as he was finished he would be out of there.

Max was shorter than average. He was skinny too, but he noticed that adults sometimes described him as 'wiry' which he had worked out meant skinny but strong. He was strong. Max had energy. He didn't walk, he certainly didn't stroll or amble - he bounced and bounded through his day. This made school lessons a chore, but football was his joy. No one ran as far, ran as fast and slid into tackles with as much effort as Max. He was the 'all action' midfielder and gave everything he could on the pitch. This energy also got him into all sorts of trouble at school.

Most teachers were not looking for an 'all action' student - they preferred quiet and diligent. So Max disliked school and school disliked him back.

He sat down and thought about what he had to do. He knew that there was no point in lying. Yes, he had been watching something on his phone but it was Poppy who was in trouble, not him. He looked at his blank page and made it spin and tumble through the air right in front of his face, as he wondered what to say. Then he caused it to fall back onto the desk.

Of course he had had his ten nuts that morning - pretty much everyone at school had, and that was the case every day.

Once you've experienced the sheer delight of seeing things move in response to your thoughts you never want to lose that ability, not even for a day.

Max had good teek skills. He could hit the bulls eye on a darts board nine times out of ten. As he sat alone in the woodwork room he looked at all the tools on the wall. In the teeking era woodwork was way more fun than it had ever been before. But that was not was Max's concern right now.

He didn't know Poppy very well. He didn't know any of the girls at school very well. Not that he disliked them - they just weren't into football enough. Or wrestling. Or farting jokes. In fact most things that were fun seemed to be things that girls weren't into, so he couldn't understand girls at all. He didn't know what Poppy had done, but he just knew that it was strange and that it was good. He wished that someone else had been there rather than him.

Because then he wouldn't have the head teacher breathing down his neck and all the pressure that this put on him. He longed for the bell to ring and put him out of this mess. If he could fast forward a couple of hours he could be in the park playing football as he would most afternoons. Right now that freedom and happiness seemed more like two years rather than two hours away.

Max hated his situation. He sighed heavily and then began to write:

> *The first thing I knew about it was when Poppy said something like, "It's right and good." I don't remember the exact words. I didn't really hear what she said but I sure do recall the way in which she said it. It wasn't girly, it wasn't soft, it was like she was in the army. I had been watching the highlights of the football on my phone. I know I shouldn't have been but I'm sorry, OK? Anyway, I had one ear bud in and Lloyd had the other, so I could hear what was being said in the room. I looked up because it was really unusual, the way that she was speaking. I looked at Poppy and she had her eyes closed. It was like she was concentrating really hard.*

> *Then Poppy yelled, "Now!" at the top of her voice. When she said it I looked at her, and she slammed her fist on the table.*

> *When she did that it felt like an earthquake. I felt it in my gut. I don't know what she did. I didn't see the table move, but something happened and I felt on the inside that the whole room had just had a tremor pass through. I've never known anything like that before.*

Then it all happened real quick. I remember that I jumped up out of my seat because I didn't know what was happening but it was like that there was electricity all around. Obviously Elz was affected by it. He was wide awake - I think he had his head down on the table before, but now he was sat bolt upright, very much awake. Then he quickly stood up and I was shocked because he doesn't move quick these days. I moved around the table towards him. I said to him, "You OK Elz?" but he didn't look at me and I don't think he heard what I said. Then he put his hands in the air, both hands, and just yelled. It was a happy yell I think - it didn't sound like he was in pain. I had no idea that he was capable of standing like that and making that kind of noise. I couldn't believe it. It was like he had been taken over by something and I had no idea what was going on. He yelled for a long time.

It was the last thing that I was expecting. I had been moving towards him but when he yelled I stopped, I might have even taken some steps backwards. I said again, "You OK mate?" but he didn't look at me or even notice me.
I decided that what was happening was so strange that I should get a teacher involved because the electricity in the room was so powerful and such crazy things were going on.

Max didn't realise that he had used the word 'electricity' when there technically was no electricity involved. It just came naturally because that's what it felt like. Max was not a complex person. He tended to form opinions quickly.

He knew if he liked someone or didn't like someone straight away. He absolutely, definitely did not like Mrs Pilot. Of that he had no doubt. But he was enjoying the small group task because he liked everyone in the group. Not that liking the people in the group caused him to want to actually do the work.

Max was a confident boy in the areas where he had strengths. He preferred to have tools or a bat and ball of any description in his hands rather than a pen. But out of his comfort zone he was shy and conservative. He didn't take risks and didn't enjoy it when things didn't go as planned. And what he was doing right now was certainly not in his plans for the day. He sighed again and continued:

> *I raced out of room 29 and into room 28 next door where Mrs Greenwood was teaching. She looked like she half expected me because I think she probably heard it when Elz screamed. I told her, "Miss, come quickly because Elz is up and I don't know what he's doing, but he might need some help."*

> *She told her class to stay in their seats and she ran into room 29 and I think I came back in after her. When we came in Elz was still on his feet and he and Poppy were hugging. He looked great. The way that he was moving was really different and it looked like he wasn't sick at all. After a few moments I caught Elz's eye and it was really weird. He was smiling the biggest smile you'll ever see someone smile and it went all the way through him. He*

was obviously really happy which was a relief because I didn't know if there was something bad happening, although I didn't think there was. It was powerful and it was weird but it never felt like it was bad.

Mrs Greenwood told Elz to sit down. He pretty much ignored her. Actually he ignored everyone - he was just happy and didn't seem in much of a mood to be taking orders from anyone. He just kept smiling and was walking around the room. He was transformed - I can't describe how different the way that he looked and the way that he moved were.

Max ran his hand through his short black hair. In between each sentence Max would tap his pen on the table, or rock back in his seat, or tap his feet to whatever tune came to mind. Anything to use up some of the energy that gushed out of him all the time. He looked at what he had written and couldn't believe how much he had said. He felt good about this. He realised there wasn't too much more to say, so he hurried on to finish the task.

After he had been walking around the room for a bit he noticed the rest of us - not Poppy, I mean. He came up to me and looked right at me, and said, "Hey Max!" and then he gave me a big hug. I hugged him and said, "man you look good." Elz said, "I feel good. I feel great man. It feels gone." Elz then spoke to the other guys as well.

Mrs Greenwood - I think she just thought she better get someone else because Elz wasn't listening to her anyway. So she went out, running. Some of the kids from room 28 decided to come in. Others were just staring from the doorway. They were staring at the six of us, and some of them were asking what had happened.

We were all really rattled. We didn't know what to do, but we knew something good had just happened. Because for Elz to go from being so sick to being so happy meant that he had had a good change.

Max felt good to have reached the end. The more he reflected on what had happened he thought that it really should be a happy occasion. Nothing seemed to be out of place. Elz was pretty clearly a whole lot healthier now than he was at the start of the day. Who knew precisely what had happened in the classroom? But what damage was done? No one was hurt, no one was upset apart from the teachers.

That made no sense - if all of the students were happy and healthy then why were all the teachers so panicked and worried? Max knew that the threat of the teek jails hovered over the situation.

They were the unspoken cloud over all their heads. But mostly Poppy's.

He made his way back to the head's office. Max spent most of his waking moments wanting to be on the football field - but right now he wanted it way more than usual.

As he walked across the school grounds to the administration block the bell sounded for the end of the day.

Max had never been so thankful for a clock reaching 3:05pm in his life. He gave his piece of writing to the lady at the main reception desk and headed for home. When he walked out of the school gate he felt free. The bounce in his step returned and it felt like a weight came off his shoulders. The school buildings were now behind him. He didn't look back.

Chapter Four

Haruka Onyo

Once teeking was discovered the world quickly raced to explore how it worked. The basic rule seemed to be that you could move anything that weighed less than yourself.

The heavier you were, the greater your ability to teek objects, and the more power you had when you were moving them. All of a sudden being overweight had a significant upside. If someone was bigger than you, then they could move you, but you couldn't move them. This changed the whole dynamic of high school bullying. Fat kids were no longer at risk of bullying - they had the ability to fight back and win.

The skinny kid was at the biggest risk - they had to be creative because everyone could move them around but they couldn't do it back.

To be able to move something you had to be able to see it. Even if you knew it was there it didn't matter - it had to be visible. If it was behind glass or clear plastic you could still teek it - as long as you could see it. You had to be able to see it clearly, however. Something vague behind frosted or bathroom glass would not move. If you looked at an object in a mirror it would not move. You had to be looking directly at it, and not at its reflection.

Teeking scientists (and there were fast becoming many thousands of them) were researching the possibility of teeking an object through its reflection but they had not made the breakthrough yet.

There seemed to be a limit of 30 or 40 metres beyond which you couldn't teek something. This is where some people seemed to naturally have more talent at teeking than others. There were people who could teek objects over 50 metres away, and the current world record for lifting a one kilogram weight one metre into the air was 68.55 metres, set at the third annual Teek Olympics. That feat made Ana Maria Escudero the most famous person in all of Argentina, as no one had previously bettered 65 metres. But at the other end of the spectrum there were some people who really couldn't teek anything, even 20 metres away.

The amount that you could move was proportionate to how far away you were. So you could move something that weighed the same as you if you were right next to it, but if it was 10 metres away then you couldn't.

Teeking was just innate - if you practised all day, every day, it didn't change your skills very much. Some people were just naturally better than others, and there was nothing that could be done about it. All sorts of rumours flew around about what can help you teek better. Some top teekers thought that sunbaking helped, others swore by eating peanut butter. Others favoured teeking with a heart pumping fast from vigorous exercise, whilst some put themselves into almost a trance of serenity.

The best American teeker had worn the same Hawaiian-style shirt in every competition he had entered. He was so adamant about its importance to his ability that it was common to see teekers wearing Hawaiian shirts as they took part in major competitions. All these ideas contradicted each other and none of them actually made any difference. They were just people being superstitious.

Age makes no difference to your teeking ability. A Teek Olympics final is just as likely to be contested by a 9 year old as a 99 year old, or anyone of any age in between. You don't improve or worsen as you get older. The Teek Olympics Opening Ceremony was therefore a very interesting thing when a collection of completely random people of all ages, shapes and colours would walk into the stadium. If you saw a photo of them you would never guess that they were the world's elite at anything at all.

Men and women had the same teeking abilities. Gender made no difference to how well you could teek, so all teek sports were mixed.

Once you were moving something you could apply quite a lot of force. So even though it was only under your control for the first 30 to 40 metres, it could then travel a great distance further if you moved it as much as possible. This meant that teek golf (or 'clubless golf') became extremely popular extremely quickly. Because the golf ball didn't weigh much you could teek it and send it a long way down the golf course.

Clubless players ended up quite evenly matched against the best traditional players, and there would occasionally be competitions between the best teekers and the best professionals.

The world's golf courses enjoyed a great surge of new players because all of a sudden the game was not nearly as difficult as it used to be, and you didn't need any fancy or costly equipment.

Surprisingly, you could teek something even though it was underneath something heavy.

This meant that you could often lift something heavier than yourself, as long as you were actually lifting the thing underneath it. This meant that the rule that you couldn't teek something heavier than yourself wasn't hard to get around. For example, the wooden pallets that are used to transport goods in trucks and on forklifts all over the world can be teeked, and whatever goods are on top will come as well, regardless of how heavy they are. It used to be impossible to think of a warehouse without a forklift. Now all you need is a packet of macadamias for each staff member.

Because of this, things heavier than yourself could be moved if they were held in a harness or anything lighter than yourself. All you had to do is teek the harness, and all of a sudden the car that it is holding is soaring through the air.

This also means that a person, even someone much heavier than yourself, could be moved or at least pushed if you teeked the jacket or backpack that they were wearing.

Teeking worked just as well on living things - it made no difference if the object of your attention was a desk, a cat or your little sister. Except of course that only one of these has the ability to complain to your mother if you teeked them.

If two people were both teeking the same object at the same time that's when things started to get interesting. It turned into a straight tug-o-war between the two people. The person who had the greater innate teeking ability would eventually win, and move the object to where they wanted it to go. Ability and body weight both reflected who would win a teek-o-war, as they began to be called. But teeking required intense concentration, and to do it for an extended period of time was not easy.

So a teek-o-war was a battle of concentration as much as innate ability. Teek-o-wars were organised into weight classes in the same way that boxing and weightlifting are. But the best ones to watch were the monster truck battles that the Americans had come up with. Two teams of fifty teekers each would stand either side of a truck.

There would be a line five metres on one side of the truck, and another line five metres on the other side. When the whistle sounded, both teams, who had to stay behind their respective lines, attempted to teek the truck towards them and get it across their line. It was a brutal test of group concentration.

The teams were made up of people who looked like sumo wrestlers, and would come up with elaborate strategies to win.

To begin with it was just some fun, but then people worked out that they could pull parts of the truck off, and dismantle the machine piece by piece. And once you had removed a door, for example, you could have one player move the door around, and block the view of the truck that the opponent's best player had.

Others worked out that if everyone, in response to a signal, moved one end of the truck, that would jerk it around and cause the other team to lose concentration. If they were thrown off for just a few seconds that is all that it might take. Monster truck teek-o-war was now a major professional sport, with superstars earning big money.

You couldn't teek yourself. For some reason when you looked at your arm, your toe or any part of your body it just would not budge an inch. Even the hairs of your arm cannot be teeked. However, you can teek something that's underneath you. So if you are sitting on, say, a surfboard, then you can teek the surfboard. The fact that you are on top of it won't stop it from moving. So it will move with you on it. And because you are still on top of it, you can continue to teek it, as it moves around.

This means that teek flying works. As long as you are sitting on an object that weighs less than you, then you can fly, for as long as your concentration holds. If your concentration doesn't hold, then gravity takes over. If you make that mistake once you generally don't get the chance to make it again. The first person to teekfly the English Channel was the great Japanese teeker Haruka Onyo.

Her amazing attempt caused an annual tradition to be established - the Channel Teeking, which draws tens of thousands of teekers from all around the world. It is 21 miles from Calais in France to Dover in the UK, and it takes around an hour to teekfly it.

That is around the absolute limit for how long the best teekers can concentrate hard enough to keep a surfboard, or whatever item they are lying on, in the air. 90% of those who attempt the Channel Teeking have to be pulled out of the water.

But for the other 10% a completion certificate is something that they would display prominently in their home. And the winner's medal would make you famous. Onyo had three.

Haruka Onyo was the greatest extreme teeker. Part of her appeal is that ordinarily she was the most modest, conservative and gentle looking Japanese housewife you might ever come across. But she combined great natural teeking abilities with amazing concentration, remarkable bravery and a surprising flair for publicity. She had pushed the boundaries of teeking where others hadn't dared. Her teekflight through the ash being spewed by a live volcano brought her to the world's attention.

But it was the 'edge of space' teekflight that had the whole planet watching. Some people gave her a 10% chance of surviving. In a specially made high altitude balloon she reached heights that few have reached before. Equipped with a special oxygen mask, a close fitting thermal suit for warmth and a modified teek surfboard strapped to her chest, she then teeked herself a further 15 miles straight up. It was easily the highest any non-astronaut has ever been.

With no parachute at all she fell for five minutes, breaking the speed of sound, and then began to teekfly, slowly arresting her descent. The whole thing worked perfectly and she even landed gently, right on the target set up in a packed Tokyo football stadium.

When you move an object you have a great deal of control over where it goes. So you can be quite precise. Teeking has completely changed the way that people move things around their houses - ladders are used much more rarely because if the suitcase needs to be put on top of the cupboard then you just look at it, and up it goes. Even if it has a very tight fit you can teek it in with a great deal of accuracy.

Similarly to golf, one game that was all of a sudden a great deal easier was darts. Almost anyone could teek a dart into the exact part of the board that they wanted. Quickly some changes were made to keep the game as a challenge - the board was reduced in size to make it harder. But more importantly the board was made of much firmer material.

This meant that the only way the dart would stick was if it was really sent flying at a significant speed. Of course the faster that it went the harder it was to control the accuracy. But like many sports teek darts suffers from a simple problem - anyone who is within 30 or 40 metres of the board can give a little nudge to the dart as it is moving. For this reason the rules of the game now insist that the player who is not throwing has to sit behind a screen so that they cannot see the darts of the player who is throwing.

While this works well enough for players who are playing professionally, many a game at home or in a pub has been marred by accusations that one of the people watching has caused a dart to change course ever so slightly.

But the great mystery for the teek scientists was why macadamia nuts made it work. Every other nut had been tried - the chemical analysis done on the macadamia over the last 10 years was incredible. Yet for everything that was known it remained a mystery. The nuts most closely related to the macadamia didn't work. Everything that anyone had made that tried to replicate a macadamia nut didn't work.

Different kinds of macadamias all worked the same. There were no better varieties that improved your teeking compared to others. There just seemed to be no substitute for macadamias and no one really knew why they allowed people to teek, or what was so special about them.

The research had been so fruitless that teek scientists themselves were becoming a bit of a joke. How many teek scientists does it take to change a lightbulb? A hundred - one to change the bulb and 99 to explain in big words that they have no idea how it happened. Of course changing a lightbulb itself was just one household job among many that was done differently to how it used to be.

But for Michael, Max, Lloyd and Jake and their fellow high school students, none of them cared about the failures of teek scientists. Not even Lloyd, whose father was a teek scientist. None of them cared how or why teeking worked. They just knew that life with 10 macadamias for breakfast each morning had way more possibilities for fun than life without them. So every day they ate up, and every day they teeked away.

Chapter Five

Lloyd

L loyd was a good student. He was the tallest of the group, and had that 'I've had this tall body for such a short time that I don't really know what to do with it' awkwardness. He would lose it in years to come, but right now he looked a foot taller than what he wanted to be, and the pimples, messy brown hair and hunched shoulders didn't enhance his appearance. But on the inside he was a team player, and no one had a bad word to say about him. Lloyd generally went through his day hoping he was doing the right thing by his parents, by his teachers, by his friends and anyone else. Most of the time he was nervous that he was falling short, but he had no idea that in fact almost everyone who knew him liked him and thought highly of him.

He liked Poppy. He thought that she had a kind of head-girl-in-waiting personality, meaning that she was likeable enough but at the end of the day she was pretty serious. He didn't want to chase after her romantically.

For Lloyd that kind of girl was just a bit too intense. But then if he ever got the idea that she might have been interested in him, he probably would have revised that view pretty fast. Because deep down he thought that she was a good catch.

Lloyd really felt for Elz as they had been good friends before he got sick. For the last year Elz was so unwell that his friends had faded off the scene to a large extent. Not because they didn't care - and Lloyd did care - but because the family had closed pretty tightly around Elz. There wasn't much possibility for Lloyd to be involved. And so friends like Lloyd simply did other things to fill their days. It wasn't a calculated decision, it wasn't a slight that they resented the family for. It was just how things were, and for teenage boys that was no drama. It was just what happened, and no one thought too much about it.

Lloyd was sent to one of the science rooms. Mr Gladstone was teaching a class, but there were no other places to put him, so Lloyd had to write his account of what happened with the distraction of the Year Seven lesson going on in front of him.

They found a desk at the back of the room and dragged it away from the others, and turned it so that he was looking at the side of the room rather than the front. It wasn't ideal but it would have to do. Lloyd had his blank page in front of him. He made his pen dance and twirl right above the top of the page where he had to start writing. As a level headed guy Lloyd didn't agonise over what to say. He realised he had to say it straight. He began:

> *About this time last year Elz got told that he had cancer. I know that it has been hard for him. They say that he is in*

remission, but it doesn't look good long term. It will probably come back, and all the treatment he has had might not get him through. So that was where he was at before our lesson today.

Poppy was stuck in a group work task with five of us boys. I don't know why it worked out that way but it was just her and the five of us. Well the four of us really because Elz wasn't really going to contribute anything to the group - it's just a bonus for him that he is well enough to come to school at all.

So Miss made us go into room 29, and we were meant to be working. We did some work at the start of it all, but then we had got distracted by other things going on. I was watching some stuff on Max's phone, some football, and Max and I were sharing an ear bud. Poppy was at the other end of the bunch of tables with Elz and Michael. I wasn't watching them really - I had my eyes on the football on Max's phone. I know that Poppy said something in a loud voice but to be honest I just didn't care because I was enjoying what Max and I were doing. It didn't sound like anything was wrong, so I didn't do anything about it.

That had been a hard paragraph for Lloyd to write because he hated admitting he was not doing what he was meant to be doing. He realised that there was no way to avoid it, and kept reminding himself that he wasn't the one who was in trouble. He just wished that Elz had got better when they were actually doing some work, half an hour before he did.

Lloyd paused as he struggled how to compose his next paragraph. He was a matter-of-fact kind of guy - how do you put into words something bizarre that he had never experienced before? How do you describe something so spooky and yet so glorious? And keep it realistic? Lloyd was a bit of a perfectionist and tended to agonise over getting his schoolwork just right. His pen hovered out of habit as Lloyd searched for the right words.

> Then there was like a tremor. It wasn't an earth tremor, but it was like a people tremor. It was a ripple that came out from the other end of the table and it went right through you. It went through the room.

Lloyd looked at that paragraph and rolled his eyes. A people tremor? What sort of nonsense was that? He would have to do better or else he would be a joke.

> When I say a tremor, I don't know what it was. But whatever it was it sure got a reaction. Elz jumped up out of his seat, and then things happened real fast. Elz was smiling a big smile - I mean he grinned like he was free, or he was happy all the way through his body.

Happy all the way through his body? Lloyd kicked himself and wondered what to say next. Then he realised that he could talk about what didn't happen, and that would be easier. He continued:

> *When it all happened no one was teeking anything. I didn't see anything move and no one was trying to do anything unusual or anything illegal. The three of them at the other end of the table were all just sitting there before it all erupted, and there was no reason to think that anything wrong was going on. In any case the three of them all get on well. Poppy likes Elz and she gets on fine with him. She likes him - not as in she has a crush on him - but they are friends and they are happy in each other's company.*

> *But when it all went off, Poppy and Elz were hugging. Then Elz noticed the rest of us, and he gave each of us a big hug like the football players do when they score a goal. He was really happy - just super smiling and grinning. Not once did I think that anyone had done anything wrong. What was bad about what had just happened? Nothing that I could see.*

> *Then Miss came in and was worried that something had gone wrong. That was the first time that it had occurred to me that anything wrong might have happened. Up until that moment I just knew that everyone was so happy because this tremor had seemed to release Elz from being so out of energy. I don't know why she thought that it was anything other than brilliant that Poppy had done what she did, because it was all Poppy making it happen.*

Miss told Elz to sit down, but he didn't really listen to her. He was too happy. He didn't care. She looked at all of us suspiciously, but there were just happy people in the room apart from her. Miss then said that she was going to get an ambulance or something, which just struck me as the last thing that anyone in the room needed. Why would you see people feeling great and think to get an ambulance?

Lloyd felt bad to have criticised one of his teachers. He tried hard to not publicly say anything bad about anyone. But he wanted it to be clear that the response to what happened was the opposite to what it should have been. He realised that he just needed to write a bit about what was said afterwards and then he was done. He was enjoying this task more than he thought he would. It was quite enjoyable to give your view without having anyone disagree with you as you are doing it.

Completely oblivious to the racket of the Year Seven lesson around him he kept writing:

But after Miss left the room to do that or whatever she did, I spoke with Poppy and asked her what happened. Poppy said that she had felt so sad because Elz was probably going to die. Then before she knew anything else she just felt full of power. And then she said that the power came out of her and into Elz and he was better. I said, "Did you teek him or something?" She just said, "No, well, I don't know. It wasn't teeking but it was something else. It was something I've never done before. I just don't know. But it was like teeking - but it wasn't me concentrating. It was me being moved by the sadness and changing it into power. At least I think it was - that's what it felt like." I said to her that it was pretty awesome. Because it obviously was.

Lloyd wanted the head in no doubt that what had happened was good, and that Poppy was the new school hero if she was anything at all. But he feared. People were super sensitive about teeking other people, and Poppy's actions could be misunderstood.

Then Lloyd realised that he had been so engrossed in writing his account of what happened that he had forgotten all about the Year 7 lesson happening right in front of him. He looked up to see the Year 7 kids heading out the door. The school day had ended, and Mr Gladstone came up to check on him. He gave sir what he had written.

Lloyd began to wander home, not knowing what to make of his day. Dark clouds were overhead as he went down the hill towards his house. There was rain coming. Lloyd realised that he had been sent to the head's office, was possibly in trouble, that Poppy might get imprisoned or excluded or both, and that everyone was talking about him and the others who were in that room. Yet despite all of that, he could not shake the feeling that this had been the best day he had ever enjoyed at school. He didn't know it but as he was walking he was smiling broadly.

His friend who was fighting a losing battle with cancer seemed to be well. He had felt something beautiful, mysterious and powerful when the tremor went through the room. It was an experience that he wasn't looking for, and certainly wasn't expecting as he sat in room 29, but it had filled him with joy. Not happiness, which comes and goes, but joy which is a deeper and more permanent thing. As he walked, for no particular reason, he teeked a small rock down the path ahead of him. His smile was still broad, but as he looked up the rain was surely just a few moments away.

Chapter Six

Ernesto Pontes

Teeking changed a huge number of things about ordinary life. But it didn't change human nature. Since humans have existed there has been love, kindness, duty, sacrifice and service. And there has also been jealousy, greed, theft, rage and revenge.

Teeking has been used to do some beautiful things. There have been some examples of teeking saving lives. The most obvious was the fire in Rio de Janeiro, Brazil, two years ago. Due to an electrical fault a fire began on the third floor of an apartment tower. Before long the stairwells were on fire, the lifts no longer worked and the whole middle of the building was ablaze. The flames were rapidly going up and up, and for those on the higher floors there was no hope. With no way of escape they were doomed to either perish by the fire or leap to their deaths.

A nearby resident, Ernesto Pontes, gathered together a group of people who had all had some nuts that day. The group of about 20 braved the heat and the danger of falling objects to gather around the base of the building. Their own lives were at risk for every minute that they stood there.

Over the next half an hour 81 people jumped off the upper floors of the building, and all 81 were 'caught' by Ernesto's group, without a single death. A number of the 81 were children who were thrown off by their parents, and there was even one baby. There wasn't even an injury apart from breathing in smoke. It was an amazing event - one of those rare occasions where the world comes together to celebrate bravery.

Pontes and those who helped him received numerous awards for their courage and became celebrities. Their fame was so great that Pontes was given the honour of officially opening the last Teek Olympics.

For romantics teeking has opened up all sorts of new doors to create beauty and love. One of social media's greatest hits was the video of the Chinese violinist who spent a year practising how to teekplay the violin. The reason he did it was so that he could propose to his girlfriend by playing beautiful music outside her third storey balcony. A friend of his teeked the violin up in the air near the balcony, and he held it in place. The violinist then teeked the bow up next to it and began to perfectly play a romantic piece by Mozart. As the song was playing the girl came to the window. More friends teeked up a giant bag of rose petals, which someone else cut with a knife they were teeking to get a 'rose petal rain' effect. Another friend made a video of the whole thing, including teeking the camera right up close to capture her facial expression and tears.

Then the beautifully designed 'Will you marry me?' sign was teeked up. As the girl nodded and cried, the violinist stopped playing, teeked up the engagement ring and teeked it onto her finger. To finish with, his friends then teeked him up to the balcony, he climbed on and the two of them embraced.

And that is how you end up with a wife - and 900 million views on social media.

But for every story of teeking being used for noble ends there is another of teeking causing pain.

As well as control. The desire of one person to control another has been with mankind for as long as mankind was more than one person. Governments across the world exercise control over their people - some do it pretty well, and others do not.

Some governments give people a great deal of freedom, and others do not. But when teeking came along, governments were thrown into confusion in deciding how to deal with citizens who could move things with their minds.

For a start, basic law enforcement was now harder. Within days of teeking being discovered jewellery shops were in crisis as many of their gorgeous and valuable products were floating around, and landing in people's pockets or bags. If they suspected someone had come in with the intention to steal what could they say? "Sir, you seem to be looking at some of our expensive rings." "Well, yes I am. How else am I expected to buy one?"

Pickpockets were also revelling in their new found powers. If you wanted to steal a woman's handbag across the other side of a crowded room...well, all you had to do was look at it whilst the woman was distracted. Perhaps someone might see the bag move - then you'd be in trouble! But no you wouldn't - if they were looking at it then it was just as likely that they were making it move as you were. So how do you ever prove someone guilty? It is a police officer's nightmare.

Some countries thought that the chaos teeking people might unleash was too great a risk.

A good number made macadamia nuts illegal. But the demand for them was so strong that a black market trade for them emerged in no time at all. Wherever there was money to pay for them, the nuts made their way somehow.

Most of these governments eventually gave up, and made the nuts legal. At least that way they could be taxed.

Teek laws that established certain teek crimes soon appeared. Activities such as teek flying were quickly covered by numerous rules - almost every accidental death resulted in a new collection of regulations and rules.

Many teek laws centred around teeking another person without their consent. Since you could teek someone smaller than yourself, two large people (such as, say, two high school bullies) could stand at either end of a football field. One of them could teek a small kid they wanted to give a hard time to - they could hold him in the air and laugh at him.

But then they could throw him in the air as far as they could. After 30 to 40 metres they would no longer have control - the young child would be flying through the air. But then the bully at the other end of the field would 'catch' them - meaning they would teek them as they came within 30 to 40 metres of them, and bring them back to earth. Which was of course great fun for the bullies, but completely terrifying for the student being thrown backwards and forwards. And obviously the risk of something going wrong, with serious injury or worse resulting, was very real. This was quite possibly the most fun that bullies had ever had - which made the need for laws about it even more urgent.

Teek pushing was the basic crime that the teek laws covered. In the past, to trip someone required you to get your leg right in front of theirs, or cause a person to trip over an object that they somehow couldn't see. But now if someone is annoying you, all you have to do is teek their jacket forwards and the force exerted by the clothing will make the person stumble and fall if you do it hard enough.

And if you make sure that you do it when there are lots of people around, then how will the victim ever be able to identify who pushed them? They can't. So even though teek pushing is illegal, it still happens often because it is so hard to catch the person doing it.

Of course if you want to push someone who is smaller than you then you don't need to teek their clothing - you can just look at them and teek their body. But rather than push their body you can lift it up into the air. Once this is done the person is stuck.

Because you can't teek yourself, there is absolutely nothing you can do when someone teeks you. There is no way to fight back. You could try to teek something else to block the person's view of you. But if you succeed in doing that then there is the problem that you will fall back to earth. So you wouldn't do that. Once you are in the air then you are totally reliant on the person who put you there having the good sense to bring you back down safely.

Human nature being what it is, that doesn't always happen. The crime of levitating another person without their consent carries serious penalties, often jail time.

Teek violence has had to be dealt with harshly. When fights start they can often quickly become serious if both people have had their macadamia nuts that day. If two guys start slugging it out because they have had too much to drink, that's one thing. If the same two guys start throwing each other up in the air, or start picking things up with their mind to belt the other over the head with, that's a different thing.

Then there's a good chance the loser will end up in hospital, if he survives at all. Lengthy prison sentences have been given to people who have engaged in teek violence, but it has become common regardless, because when people are fighting they are often not thinking straight.

The most serious crime of all is teek murder. Murder has been around for as long as people have been, but the more man invents, the easier it gets. Just as the gun made murder easier, teeking has made it easier again. If you are standing next to someone smaller than you, then you could teek them into the air as far as you can, and if they land on concrete they probably won't survive.

That is a temptation that some people have not been able to resist. Therefore, many countries have made laws that punish teek killers far more severely than ordinary murderers.

Then there is the threat of inside teeking. This is the name that has been given to what a small number of people have done, and it terrifies many. When you look at a person smaller than you and concentrate on them, then you can move them.

The person doesn't feel that you are 'holding' a particular part of their body or anything like that. They just feel their whole body move. But if you focus on one particular part of the person's body, then you can move just that part of the body.

So if you 'move' someone's arm, that person will get dragged along with their arm leading the way, unless they can grab on to something with their legs or their other arm to stop it. And if you focus on the arm but move it backwards rather than forwards, then the person will feel a push. It is not sharp like a punch - but it is a push, and it can be a quite strong push. That's all straightforward, but inside teeking is a technique that some have developed where you look at a person's skin, and you start pushing.

But those who have mastered this skill can apply pressure that seems to go all the way through the body. They can do internal damage to the muscles and organs. And if they look at the outside of the chest, and they apply pressure to the skin near the heart, and that pressure then goes through the heart ... then people die. Inside teeking can be used to kill.

Whilst the number of actual murders that have happened this way is very small, it scares people no end.

Horror movies now have all sorts of gruesome teeking deaths, and scary people using inside teeking are one of their staples.

As all these teek laws have been made, the principle that has emerged at the root of them all is the centrality of the body. The right of people to have complete control over their own body is at the heart of most teek laws. If you use teeking to deny someone else control of their own body then you are probably in trouble.

In the United Kingdom the age of criminal responsibility is 10 years old. That means that a nine year old cannot commit a crime. It doesn't matter what they do, how naughty they are, it is an impossibility for them to do something criminal in the eyes of the law. It might be criminal to your mind, it might drive their parents crazy, but no court will convict them. Criminal laws therefore apply to everyone age 10 and up. These rules generally don't get used much - courts hardly ever see a 10 year old, an 11 year old or anyone under 15 really. It can make headlines when they do.

But that all changed with teeking, because a mischievous 11 year old who has had their macadamia nuts that morning might choose to start pushing people around, or even throwing them around. And the law developed very strict penalties for people who did these things, even if they were very young.

At the last UK election there was great debate about teek laws, and what should happen to those who broke the law. The result of a heated debate was the construction of new prisons, built especially for people who committed teek crimes. Amidst great controversy a law was passed that anyone arrested for a teek crime of any kind must be put in a teek prison for 24 hours, in theory until the macadamia nuts that they had eaten were no longer effective.

Of course they might end up being put on trial and kept in prison for a much longer period than that. The idea was to offer a serious and immediate punishment for anyone who had teeked in the wrong way. Sure, there were some who got arrested, imprisoned and it turned out they had done nothing wrong. But that was just bad luck for them.

The government felt that teek crime was out of control and something drastic had to be done. Far from protesting in anger, the great majority of people thought that this was an excellent idea and fully supported treating teek criminals as harshly as possible. So the teek jails were deliberately awful. There were many people in each cell, the guards were rude, the toilets horrid and no one could believe that buildings so new were dilapidated so quickly and completely. All of a sudden children were a whole lot less eager to teek a schoolmate who did something nasty to them.

Teeking changed what people could do in a massive and unexpected way. But it didn't change the way they treated one another. That continued to be the same mix of good, bad, loving, hateful, warm, hostile, gracious and awful that it had always been. Moving objects was now easy. Moving the heart was as hard as ever.

Chapter Seven

Jake

Jake was sent to a vacant English classroom. He sauntered across the school grounds to get there. Jake had an uncanny ability to stand out of the mainstream without breaking a rule. The way that he cut his hair was not technically against the school rules, but it was right on the border. The way that he wore his uniform was pretty much in accordance with every single regulation about how the shirt is to be worn, how the tie is to be fastened, and how the whole package can appear. Yet he stood out a mile.

If a catch-all rule was added to the uniform code saying that looking unusual, stylish or like you just don't care was banned, then Jake would have been in trouble. He had blonde hair and wore a school blazer that was faded enough that you could pick it out easily in a group. Whilst he usually wore good looking clothes, the fact was that he had the power to make most clothes look good. Because above all the clothing and the hair were the eyes that sparkled in just the right way to make girls' hearts flutter and make the guys wish they could be him. Everything about his appearance said, "I am within the rules but the rules don't apply to me."

Of course this infuriated Mrs Pilot who just wanted him to be like everyone else. It marked him out as 'not easy to control' and those were the kinds of people that Mrs Pilot watched very closely indeed. But of course there was no rule against standing out for these reasons. So Jake stood out, and took great pleasure in doing so.

He was intrigued by what had just happened in the classroom with Poppy and Elz. It was by far the most interesting thing that had happened in a long time. It was astonishing. He was thrilled that not only had such an amazing event happened while he was there, he was now getting the chance to write it up while it was fresh in his mind. He walked into the empty classroom. His heart soared at the chance to have the whole room to himself to write.

Since there was no rule about where he had to sit he slid into the teacher's padded chair. It felt good.

He put his paper down on the desk and considered how he would approach the task. Within a moment he was deep in thought. He decided that he wanted to capture the essence of what had happened, so that whoever read it would believe the right things about Poppy.

If they got that right then Poppy's name would be protected, in fact all of them would be free and the news of the glorious thing that had happened would spread. It could lead to other people being set free just like Elz had - who knew? So he wanted to get it right, and describe Poppy as the one who did the right thing. He set to his task:

In the beginning was the warmth. The sun poured through the windows and we sat to collect its rays. It was warm in the room and it was warm around the table. Poppy was running the work that we were doing. She led it well, but there was no leader. No one was given that title, but Poppy filled the role, and she shone, and the sun shone as she did it. We did some work at the start but the sun was too strong for us, so we ended up doing different things. We fought against the sun but we didn't fight hard. It melted our resolve, and we relaxed.

In the room was Michael, Max, Lloyd, Poppy, Elz and myself. Miss had put us together to do the task on the Black Death. But with the Yellow Life so brightly coming through the window there was no way the Black Death could hold on. So it went away and other things came out. Homework came out, phones came out, football came out, and sleep came out, each of them better than the Black Death.

Michael worked on his maths homework. Everything added up for him. He filled his heart with the sun, and filled his head with the numbers.

Max and Lloyd did some of the work and then did some of the play. They sat in the beams and watched the goals go in.

Elz fell asleep because of the warmth. He rested his head and his heart was at peace because he was with his allies and there was peace all around. There was grace upon us all because Elz felt safe in our midst and he is the most vulnerable of us all. There was a rest in Elz's body and a rest in his heart because he slept in safety as we relaxed and enjoyed the sun.

I had my maths book out but the sun stopped me from doing much work. The geometry questions turned into pretty patterns, so I chased a shadow across my page and drew doodles inspired by question 7 on my homework task. The triangles turned into a stegosaurus, who then ate the first six questions. And the warmth made us all feel at peace, as we sat there together.

Jake stopped and re-read what he had just written. He was happy with it - it captured the mood just right. He pushed his stylish blonde fringe out of his eyes.

Pushing his hair was something he generally did about 200 times a day, and was a price he was more than willing to pay to have the right look. He considered what to say in the next section of his work.

After the warmth came the power. The power emerged through the sunshine when Poppy started talking. Her eyes were closed and she was not aware of what was going on around her. There was a statement - "This is right. This is fair. This is good." And then there was a time given -

"NOW!" At that moment the power came. It moved from Poppy's hand and it went through the room. It filled each of us and made us rock. I felt the power and it was unlike any previous feelings I've known. It was a feeling, a presence, a movement, an explosion without sound or fire. You knew that it was here and that it came to do what it meant to do. There was no accident, there was no coincidence, there was just power doing what it knew it was here to do.

Once the power went through the room each of us responded differently. Elz was filled with the power and he stood straight - he called out and the power came through in his voice. His voice shook the room further, and it sounded unlike him. It sounded free, and he has been captive to the disease for so long.

Poppy let the power out through her tears. I don't know if she knew how great a thing she had done, how awesome an act she had undertaken. But there was a release of emotion as she sat in the aftershock of the power.

The power caused Max and Lloyd to jump up and start moving around. Max and Lloyd were trying to see if Elz was OK but they didn't need to. Elz was obviously fantastic. Which was the whole point of the power coming.

Jake was frustrated that he couldn't do justice to what had just happened. It was so incredible. He realised that there was a lot at stake as he wrote, so he wanted to get it right.

He enjoyed writing, he enjoyed reading, he enjoyed anything creative. These were his things. He didn't care for anything that involved running around. Why sports were so popular - both playing and watching - was surely one of life's great mysteries. He knew that the other three boys would write in a similar, more mundane style.

They might say what happened but not convey the meaning behind it. And Jake knew that what had happened was important - it was not a strange random event but something that was meant to happen. He carried on:

> *After the power came the joy. Elz had the joy most of all and his smile reached all the way through everyone he looked at. His joy went into everyone else. Poppy embraced him and she shared in his joy. Now her tears were tears of joy. When the joy came fully upon Poppy, then she was smiling just like Elz was.*

> *For the four of us, we each realised that what had happened was indeed just and fair and good. We saw Elz standing, overcome with joy and we shared in his joy. We each embraced him and the smile that he was wearing came into our souls and then onto our faces. He looked well. He is well. He had gone into the room in cold, in impotence and in doom. He came out in warmth, power and joy.*

Mrs Greenwood came rushing into the room, but since she did not experience the power, she did not perceive the joy. There was no reason to not perceive the joy - it was clear as the sun that shone through the window but she rejected it nonetheless. I believe that many will perceive it because Elz will carry it with him everywhere he goes. He will tell about it and his testimony will persuade because the results cannot be argued with. Elz could not persuade her that good had been done. She left to involve others and worry over problems that didn't exist.

I wanted to stay in the room. I wish I was there right now, and that the shining sun was on me always. I don't know if the power would still be in the room if I went back there again. Even now as I write clouds have come and rain threatens. But we will always have that moment. It cannot be taken away.

Jake stopped and read over his statement. He liked it - it captured the heart of what had happened. He was still buzzing. What a great day it had been - a famous day. A day when the Black Death turned into the Brightest Joy.

Jake glanced up at the clock and saw that it was just ten minutes until the end of the school day. He took his few pages of writing and sauntered once more across the playground. He made sure that the trip was slow enough that he wouldn't have to go to class. He handed the pages over to the office, and was told to go to class. For the last two minutes of the day?

I don't think so, Jake thought to himself, as he nodded, pretending to be obedient. Instead he walked to the school gate and was the first one through as the bell rang.

A few minutes later he was walking home wishing that the dark clouds would leave and the glorious sunshine would come again and fill his heart ever higher with joy. But the clouds couldn't ruin a day as good as this. He started to dream about where it could all lead. Imagine if what had happened to him could be repeated?

Chapter Eight

Poppy

As Michael, Max, Lloyd and Jake each were writing, Mrs Pilot worked out what approach she would take. She was so experienced at this. Over her career she had caught so many lying students. The kids don't realise how obvious their lies are to a teacher who has been doing this for far longer than the student has been alive.

On this occasion, Poppy wasn't the kind of student you need to break down with trick questions - not like some courtroom drama.

It was simply about getting her account but with lots of detail. The more detail obtained meant that the lies would eventually come to the surface. The more lies you have to make up, the more chance that one of them will get exposed. From there everything unravels.

Mrs Pilot knew that the teek laws were harsh. She never imagined that she would have some of her students held in prison every now and then. But truth be told it really made the children behave. It was the strongest, sharpest incentive to good behaviour that had ever been created. And for that, she wasn't sorry - not at all. She remembered the madness of the early days of teeking - it threw a great many parts of society into chaos, but education was hit hard.

Female teachers and students had to stop wearing skirts to school, theft of school equipment went through the roof, teek violence was everywhere, and all of it was incredibly hard to police. At least those days were now in the past.

These days there was order. Or at least there was in her school, where there was no reluctance to call the police. If other head teachers were content to let the madness continue then that was their own problem. But in this part of London, in this school, the law was enforced and order was the outcome.

She made her notes ready and called out, "Poppy, come in now."

Poppy got up and stepped through the office doorway nervously. Poppy hadn't been in this office before. It was the size of the room that got her attention. It made her even more nervous, as it did every student who found themselves in trouble. Simply by being large the office said, "You have done something so wrong that you have been brought before the most important person on these premises, so you are going to face severe consequences." Poppy got the unspoken message, and she was afraid.

"Sit down Poppy" Mrs Pilot motioned to the chair in front of her large desk. Poppy sat as instructed.

"Poppy as you know", Mrs Pilot began, "there was an incident earlier this afternoon in room 29. I want you to tell me what happened, in full, not leaving anything out. Start now." Every word was spoken to convey maximum seriousness - and

Mrs Pilot could see that Poppy was anything but flippant. Mrs Pilot felt confident that she would soon be at the bottom of this.

Poppy began cautiously. "Well Mrs Pilot, we had a history lesson and we had been given this group work task on the Black Death. Like you said we were put into room 29 which wasn't being used that lesson."

Poppy had been looking down at Mrs Pilot's desk as she had been speaking. She didn't know what had happened, she didn't know how to describe it, and she certainly didn't know what you should say to the head teacher when you might be in trouble for inside teeking. She couldn't bear to look at Mrs Pilot - she had no idea what reaction her story was getting. But at the end of her first two sentences Poppy realised that the chance to talk about what happened, the chance to tell her story in full, was precisely what she needed to help process her own feelings. Because she knew she had done nothing wrong, her fear soon faded, and she began speaking faster.

She began to look Mrs Pilot in the eye, as well as up to the roof when she was searching for the right words, or to recall some detail correctly. Over the next minutes she gave her explanation of the task they had been given, of who was in the room and where they were all sitting.

Mrs Pilot took detailed notes and frequently made Poppy stop so that she could get it all down. But at the back of her mind Mrs Pilot could see that she was dealing with a student who had strength. Poppy gave her explanation clearly, and her voice carried well.

This was no mouse, but someone who knew her own mind, even though she was under intense pressure.

Once these details had been explained Mrs Pilot said, "What happened next?"

Poppy reached for the right words to describe something that bordered on the indescribable. "Well, I sat there and the sun made me sleepy, but it wasn't really sleep.

It was a feeling that it was hot, and that I couldn't concentrate on the work. So I was thinking, and I closed my eyes. I wasn't asleep, in fact I was very much awake, as the heat came through me. I had never known such heat but my heart was drawn to Elz. I couldn't stop thinking about Elz. It's so wrong what he has had to go through. I was overcome with sorrow for him - it is just awful. It's not right. I'm still moved by it, even now.

"It felt like the heat was building up inside of me. I could feel it increasing and growing, and I didn't know what to do. I wasn't thinking about anyone else in the room - in fact if they all left the room I don't think I would have noticed because I was just so focussed on Elz, and what was happening inside me. I don't know how long I was like that for. It felt like ages but I don't think that it was ages for everyone else. It was like this huge amount of warmth and compassion was building up behind the wall of a dam. It took more and more energy to hold it all in, and I realised after fighting it that I was not meant to fight it, that it needed to come out, and that was the whole purpose of my being given this power."

Poppy became more and more animated as she spoke. She lent forward in her chair, and she spoke faster still.

"And then I just let it out. The dam wall failed, I guess. It came flowing out of me - exploding out of me - and it was way more powerful than what I thought it was. It came out and I was speaking loudly but I can't even recall what I said. It just was this huge amount of heat that came out from me and was directed at Elz. And then it was gone. It was over, and I felt exhausted. I felt like I had just run a marathon.

I noticed that Michael, Max, Lloyd and Jake were all wide-eyed and didn't know what was going on. But that was just really out of the corner of my eye because I looked at Elz and he was on his feet! On his feet! I knew that it had worked, that he's good now. I got up and I hugged him because he looked so happy. I was happy too. I was so happy that I was crying.

"I know that he's well. I know that he's not sick anymore. I don't know why I know that but I would bet my life that it's true. It's awesome."

In these conversations Mrs Pilot normally maintained an as-intimidating-as-possible facial expression. But that was long gone. Mrs Pilot simply looked blank because she had no idea what to make of it - she had never heard anything like this ever before.

Poppy lent back in the chair and paused before continuing, "Then after that Mrs Greenwood came in, and she tried to work out what was happening. But she didn't get it.

And that was just half an hour or an hour ago, I guess. Mrs Greenwood told me to come down here. So that's what happened."

Mrs Pilot had to remind herself that she was trying to deal with this situation. It was such a compelling story she had gotten lost in the wonder of it. She was trying to work out what to ask next but her overwhelming thought was that this is just remarkable.

Quickly she remembered where she was. She said, "So Poppy, you've said nothing about teeking just now."

There was an uncomfortable silence. Mrs Pilot deliberately left the sentence hanging there, without asking a question. She was leaving it for Poppy to fill in the space, to get the details she wanted. Poppy let the silence grow. Then Poppy simply said, "No, I haven't."

Mrs Pilot was frustrated that this was not going how these interviews normally do. She increased her volume, even though it was not needed, and said, "Well, were you teeking in the middle of all this or were you not?"

Poppy paused as her thoughts came together. "No, it wasn't teeking."

Then Mrs Pilot asked, "Did you have mac nuts this morning?"

Poppy replied, "Yes. I do every morning."

But what surprised Mrs Pilot was that Poppy held her eyes as she said this. She had lost count of the number of times that a student had denied teeking, and then when asked if they had eaten nuts that day their eyes go straight to the floor as they acknowledge that they had.

But Poppy looked her straight in the eye as she answered.

From there the interview didn't last too much longer. There wasn't a great deal more that Poppy had to say, and they were soon going around in circles.

Poppy felt immense relief as she left the large office. Within minutes she had the same feeling again as the school day ended. She headed for home as fast as she could. As she walked through the corridors and across the playground she knew that people were looking at her. She could tell that word was spreading fast that she was in trouble for what had happened. She didn't want to talk to anyone about it. She just wanted to be home, and to forget that high school existed. As fast as her legs could go she left school. She knew that her phone was buzzing with messages from her friends asking a hundred questions. She ignored everything and raced home.

Half an hour later Mrs Pilot reclined in her chair, with the four boys' writings in front of her. A few minutes earlier she had spoken to Poppy's mother on the phone.

She had told her that an incident had occurred which was being investigated, and there would be further news about it in the next few days.

As she looked from one account to the other she was surprised. Michael, Max, Lloyd and Jake had made similar claims. She wondered what on earth Jake would end up doing with his life, but that was not important right now.

She didn't think that they had colluded, nor did they have any incentive to mislead - they were not in trouble themselves. Poppy's story seemed to be very much in the same vein as well. So she deemed their accounts to be accurate descriptions of what had happened.

She thought that what had occurred in room 29 was a mystery but it was a very strange mystery. The first thing that surprised her about it all was that nothing bad seemed to have happened. If anything, it was something good.

Her thoughts were interrupted by a knock on the door. Her personal assistant came in straight after knocking, without waiting for a response.

"Ma'am, Eleazar's parents have just called. They are at the hospital. He is under observation. He seems to be fine.

But he's clearly way better than he has been, and no one knows why. There is no problem that they can see at the moment. I will keep you updated."

"Okay. Thank you." Mrs Pilot replied. The assistant left.

That confirmed it. There just didn't seem to be anything wrong, anything misplaced, anything against any rule. The possibility remained that Eleazar was now well. As in, healed of cancer. But that would be impossible.

Yet, everything that people thought was possible about how the human body works was spectacularly turned on its head ten years ago.

"Was this a teeking incident?", she asked herself.

That was the big question. On one hand, what has happened here is so exceedingly strange that it must be a teeking thing. If there was no teeking, then how could any of these crazy things have happened? But on the other hand what actually moved? Teeking is simply moving things with your mind, it is not a description of everything unusual or unexplainable in the world.

Poppy's school record was on her desk as well. A quick glance confirmed her hunch - a fine student, no teeking incidents on record. Just the kind of student you wish you could clone really.

The rain started to fall on her office window as the afternoon went on. She was lost in her thoughts. It was a tricky situation that she faced. Under the regulations as the school head, it is her decision as to whether charges are pressed against Poppy.

If she decides that a teeking incident has occurred then Poppy would be arrested and imprisoned that very day.

The following day the police would decide what to do next. So she could conclude that it was a teeking incident and contact the police.

She had done it before. More than once. Most head teachers had. But not to a student like Poppy. How would she even describe it to the police? What moved?

Nothing that she could tell. But something, well, in the boys' words, something powerful happened. And it seemed to have changed things for Eleazar.

She leaned towards not calling the police. She had on her hands a mystery, not a teek crime. Just because teeking is now part of life doesn't mean that every mystery is a teeking incident. Some things just have explanations that are beyond us. For the moment this was one such event. So she would not contact the police, and would wait to hear further about how Eleazar was doing.

There was another knock on her door, and her personal assistant appeared again. "Ma'am, you are going to want to see this." The assistant placed a piece of paper in front of her. It was a print out of Eleazar's social media account. The most recent post was at the top of the page. It read:

> *"I feel awesome!!!!! Today at school Poppy teeked me free of cancer. I am 100% better. YES!!!!"*

The blood drained from Mrs Pilot's face. "Oh no" she said, without realising it. The print out showed that the post was just 60 minutes old but already it was being shared widely. Reactions and comments were pouring in.

Her assistant added, "Ma'am, a couple of parents have called in the last ten minutes to ask what has happened with this incident. As you know, under the teek regulations we have to call a public meeting if there has been a teeking incident at the school."

"Yes, I know." Mrs Pilot realised that her plan to deal with it tomorrow was hopeless. Events were moving far more quickly than she could control. She needed to act.

"Okay - call a meeting for 7pm tonight. Send out the usual messages to the entire school community." She mentally reorganised her evening, and prepared to be in full head teacher mode for a few more hours yet. She didn't mind.

Mrs Pilot had chaired many such meetings, but this one would be different. She looked at the four accounts on her desk again. Elz might have said that Poppy teeked, but Mrs Pilot just didn't think that she had.

Chapter Nine

Mrs Pilot

At 3:30pm the automated message went out to the parents of all of the school's 800 or so students. The staff began to fill the hall with chairs. Mrs Pilot phoned Poppy's mother and spoke again, this time telling her to come this evening.

There was no mistaking the sense of panic in Mrs Joshua's voice. She knew that what she was hearing meant that her daughter might end up spending the night in jail. It was a genuine possibility.

The parents of the four boys who had been in the room were also informed directly. They said that they would be there.

It was now 4:30pm. Solid rain was coming down on the office windows. The office might have intimidated Poppy a few hours earlier but it was the hall full of parents that would intimidate Mrs Pilot. She wondered how things were unfolding online.

She considered for a moment that it might not be a good idea to enquire. It would probably be wise just to stay professional and do the right thing by the regulations. Don't get caught up in what someone silly on the other side of the world was saying, she told herself. But she couldn't resist. She called out to her assistant. "Julia, just give me a brief update on what's happening social media wise."

A few minutes later Julia came in to the office. "Well ma'am, Eleazar might be under observation in the hospital but that hasn't stopped him being active on his phone. Him and tens of thousands of others.

His earlier post seems to be the biggest talking point in the country right now. I think over 200 of our students have commented. Some parents have expressed concern. I think this will get the attention of the authorities."

"Oh no. Tell them to put extra chairs out in the hall." Then as much to herself as to Julia she said, "This whole thing is snowballing and it only happened this afternoon."

"Yes ma'am."

Mrs Pilot reached for her copy of the Education Department's summary of the new teek laws. There could be no mistake. There would be no mistake. If a head teacher handles something like this poorly it can destroy them. With the eyes of the whole school community on her, she wasn't going to slip up tonight. She wasn't having some minor breach of the rules wash away the career that she had spent 30 years building.

Lloyd was the first of the boys to become aware that there would be a meeting tonight. His mother got the message and asked him about it straight away. He started messaging the others before his mother had finished talking to him. He couldn't believe it. They couldn't believe it either.

The post that Elz had put on social media a couple of hours ago was still receiving a huge amount of comment and shares, especially from the school community. The news of the meeting tonight meant another round of comments. So Jake jumped on and said,

"The meeting tonight is a complete joke. Poppy should be thanked, not punished. So if you think that Elz getting better is a good thing, meet at Poppy's place on Woodland Terrace at 6:30 tonight and we will walk to school together. Pilot is a joke - Poppy deserves our support!"

Jake knew that there was every chance that "Pilot is a joke" would get him into trouble. He didn't care. He would stand up for his friend and for what was right. Within minutes Jake's comment had a life of its own. All sorts of people said they would come.

Some were students who agreed with Jake. And some were friends of students who agreed with Jake.

And some were friends of those friends and they didn't really know if they agreed or not, but if you were against Pilot then they were in. Others didn't know Jake at all but it all sounded a bit interesting, so they decided they would come along as well.

A bit over an hour later a crowd started building in the middle of Woodland Terrace, which was a mystery to the residents there. Before too many minutes had passed the crowd had grown, and was now well into the hundreds.

Woodland Terrace was an ordinary street in Charlton, in the South East of London. Poppy had lived there for many years, with her mum, and her little brother James, and her little sister Olivia. The first that Poppy knew that anything was going on was when James called out, "Why are there lots of people outside?" Her mother wandered over to the window. "What on earth!" she called out in shock.

Poppy had been in her bedroom, lying on her bed and dreading the meeting that would come later tonight. She was wishing that she could vanish, but the note of surprise in her mother's voice made her get up and look out the window.

She couldn't believe it. There must have been several hundred students from her school out there. And loads of other people as well. The street was totally blocked to traffic.

She instantly knew that they were all waiting for her.

Michael, Max, Lloyd and Jake had pushed their way through the crowd to be right next to Poppy's door. They were bossing around anyone who might try to take charge and everyone else they thought might need some bossing.

They looked at the huge crowd with delight. This would be a proper march - a great way to make a statement to the school. It was raining but that didn't seem to have put people off.

Ten minutes later Poppy opened the door. There was a roar from the crowd. They started chanting, "Poppy, Poppy, Poppy!" Poppy emerged from the door and look confused. Her eyes were wide as she took in the vast crowd. There was still enough sunlight for every second person to have their phone out and be filming or taking photos.

The four boys right in front of her were beaming. Tears hit the back of Poppy's eyes as she looked at them. She hugged each in turn and said, "Thank you so much. Thank you for being on my side." Poppy's mother, Miriam, ventured outside as well, not knowing what to make of it all. It was normally a ten minute walk to school. But after they had both taken it all in Miriam said to Poppy, "Better head off darling - not sure we will get there as fast as usual tonight."

But at that moment Michael decided that a speech was called for. He turned to Max and Lloyd and said, "Teek me up. I'm gonna say some stuff."

A few seconds later Michael rose into the air and shouted to the crowd, "Listen up! Listen up everyone! This is Poppy's victory march - we are walking to school tonight to celebrate that Elz is free of cancer and Poppy is the one who did it. So Poppy, lead us off - we don't want to keep Mrs Pilot waiting!" More chanting of "Poppy! Poppy! Poppy!" broke out, and Poppy reluctantly started towards school. The four boys made sure Poppy was at the head of the crowd, and they walked alongside her. The rain was steady but people teeked their umbrellas into the air above Poppy to keep her dry.

Fifteen minutes later the crowd reached the school gate. Michael made sure that they would arrive with enough noise so that everyone coming to the meeting knew that Poppy had plenty of support. Poppy felt grateful for what the boys had done, but she knew they were no longer in control.

Her fate was now in different hands and they were not as friendly as those she had marched with.

At 7pm the hall was heaving. Hundreds of students, hundreds of parents, and an atmosphere that was tense and hostile. The party feel that the march had enjoyed was completely gone. Once inside the school hall a different feeling took hold.

Everyone could feel the awkwardness, everyone could feel the stress. Poppy and her mother sat in the front row.

Miriam was white as a ghost. Poppy herself looked like she wanted to cry. The thought that this whole meeting was happening because of her was horrifying.

Michael, Max, Lloyd and Jake were also sat in the front row. Their parents were present but the four boys worked it so that they were sitting next to each other. All four of them were appalled by what was happening. They each knew, and were convinced, that whatever had happened this afternoon was something to be celebrated. It called for a party, not throwing someone in jail. They didn't know what they could do, but if they could help Poppy at all they would do it.

Many of the parents were anxious. They chatted amongst themselves, and most of the chatter was about keeping their children safe from teeking without their consent. The thought of students teeking one another as they played some game of doctors and nurses terrified them. It had accidental death written all over it. Whilst there was a range of views about what had happened, the parents shared an intense desire that their children be kept safe from any student attempt to do inside teeking. Even if it was done from a desire to help.

There were many other school staff present in the meeting but Mrs Pilot knew that this moment was all about her. This was her moment to prove herself in the eyes of the whole school community, over a matter of the utmost seriousness. She would not trip up. The clock reached 7pm. Starting precisely on time showed her professionalism. She strode to the microphone.

"Ladies and gentlemen, thank you for coming out this evening. Please take your seats. I have called this meeting to address an incident that happened this afternoon."

In a clear and crisp style she explained to the parents who was being investigated. She explained that Eleazar was under observation in the hospital, but all signs were that he was OK. She explained the way that she had dealt with it this afternoon.

Then came the bit that mattered. She had written out what she was going to say word for word. She knew that reading from prepared remarks was less effective as a way to communicate, but she did not want a single word out of place. There was too much at stake. She read aloud:

"Having read the accounts of Michael, Max, Lloyd and Jake, and having spoken to Poppy at length, I have formed the view that what happened today was not a teeking incident."

A strong murmur went around the entire hall. Poppy and her mother breathed a massive sigh of relief. The four boys pumped their fists and smiled. Mrs Pilot continued reading from her notes: "I note that firstly, nothing moved. Secondly, no one was harmed. Thirdly, Poppy had her eyes closed at the significant moments. So whilst we are not sure precisely what did occur, it does not appear to involve teeking, and I do not propose to call the police."

Ripples of noise moved across the hall. A hundred people spoke at once, some in whispers but others unafraid to be heard. One father jumped to his feet and loudly said, "What about inside teeking? Surely that's what this is!"

Mrs Pilot was aghast. It was not the fact that someone had disagreed with her decision. It was the fact that the meeting was only ten minutes old, and already people were speaking out of turn. These were British people. They are life-long experts at waiting their turn and forming orderly queues. The fact that the meeting was so strongly against her so early on concerned Mrs Pilot greatly.

Mrs Pilot answered, "I, of course, have considered that it might be inside teeking. However, on balance, there is simply no evidence of any harm to Eleazar. It's true we don't know what the doctors are seeing right now, but if it turns out that he has been harmed then I can change my view and report the matter to the authorities. There is nothing to be gained by being premature, and nothing to be lost by waiting." It was a good answer, and she knew it. Yet it seemed to bounce off the meeting without making any impact at all.

Another parent spoke without being invited to. "If you don't crack down on this they will all be trying to do it to each other, and what's that going to lead to? It will be chaos, and someone's going to get hurt." Many voices murmured in approval. Before Mrs Pilot could reply someone else was on their feet.

"If you can't ensure that this school is safe for our children, we will have to take them somewhere else." A great number of voices rose in agreement.

Mrs Pilot was determined to keep control. She figured that a display of strength was what was called for.

People respect the leader who stays their course under pressure. That leader is not always liked but they are respected. And Mrs Pilot was determined to be respected.

Speaking loudly she said, "Ladies and gentlemen I insist that people ask questions through the microphone being held by Mr Grayson down the front of the hall here. I will not allow speaking out of turn to create disorder. Now, in response to the comments just made, I say again that after careful consideration of four pieces of written evidence plus an extended interview with Poppy herself, I find no basis for a charge of inside teeking. The school is safe. The children are not allowed to teek at school. So I therefore do not propose to involve the police." Then, with a great sense of foreboding, she invited questions from the floor.

All her lecturing just seemed to raise people's emotions higher, rather than bring them down. There were questions about what the teachers should have done, questions about what the laws required, questions about the way in which she had handled it.

For the whole time the mood stayed hostile, and Mrs Pilot kept her two hands on either side of the lectern. She felt like she was riding a bull at the rodeo, but she was determined that she would remain in control. Her hands gripped the lectern and her leadership kept the meeting in order. Just.

When it seemed like most of the questions that had been asked were asked, a new voice spoke up. A father who everyone knew worked as a lawyer said,

"Mrs Pilot have you notified the authorities that a child had been hospitalised as a result of an accident at school?"

Mrs Pilot paused. Her mind raced. That was a requirement under the Education Department's ordinary rules. It had nothing to do with teeking laws, just ordinary ones that had been around for years. In the rush to work out whether a teeking incident had occurred, no one had thought of the ordinary laws that applied as well. Elz went to the hospital every week for check ups and monitoring even when he was doing OK. No one had thought of the need to let the authorities know that he was there. She answered slowly, "No, I have not. My priority has been to investigate the possibility of a teeking incident." People generally seemed content with that answer. But Mrs Pilot was concerned. The man who asked the question then looked at another parent across the room who was looking back. This man, who was also a lawyer, then asked the next question.

"Mrs Pilot, if students are doing things to each other that are putting them in hospital, then surely the least you can do is follow the correct procedures?" The parents murmured in agreement.

Such a simple question - in the midst of people fighting for their lives in hospital could the head teacher not at least follow some standard procedures? Surely that is not too much to ask?

Mrs Pilot answered that she was committed to following the right procedures, and noted that the incident had only happened a few hours ago. But then this parent looked to a third parent, again a lawyer and a mother, who rose to speak.

Mrs Pilot neared a state of panic. This was organised, and she was helpless to stop where this line of questioning was going.

"Mrs Pilot, you know that I have suffered greatly because of a teeking accident." The woman now speaking, Mrs Priestly, had indeed suffered, and the whole school community knew it. Her youngest child had died two years ago when some children were teeking each other. It was never clear what precisely had happened in that accident, but as a mother she had gone through pain that others could only guess at. Mrs Pilot was also aware that right now this made her the ideal person to mount an argument that would get the school to change its course of action. The woman continued, "I am very concerned about what happened today. I never want another parent to go through what I have been through. I never want anyone to suffer as I have. I believe that the only way we can prevent further tragedies is by firm and decisive action. That is why the teek laws were passed, and it now falls to you, Mrs Pilot, to protect our children. I don't care what this child's motives were. I care that a child is in hospital, fighting for his life, and my child's school is not following basic procedures, is not planning to report the incident, and I fear that if a firm message is not sent tomorrow, the whole playground will be an ocean of children teeking one another in some sort of attempt to copy what happened today. There must not be another mother like me who is robbed of their family because laws were not obeyed."

Mrs Priestly's voice now rose as she neared her conclusion. She took off her mother's hat, so to speak, and put on her lawyer's one.

"Let me be clear - if you do not report this as a teeking incident I will file a formal letter of complaint with the Education Department for your failure to comply with the law, your failure to protect our children and your failure to perform the basic tasks of your job. For the sake of our children I urge you to act now." The meeting erupted in a long, loud, sustained applause.

Those clapping were not upset with Mrs Pilot a few minutes ago, but they had been persuaded by the lawyers and Mrs Priestly. The risk was great, and the law must be followed. Mrs Priestly knew what happened when it wasn't, and that must be avoided at all costs. If that meant jail for Poppy then so be it.

Mrs Pilot looked out and knew that she must change course. Perhaps she was persuasive before, but Mrs Priestly's perfectly delivered speech had swept the meeting away from her. If Mrs Priestly lodged the complaint it may or may not amount to anything. Who could tell? But in the court of public opinion she would be ruined. Her reputation would never recover, and her hold on her position would be undermined. She might hold on to her job, but it would be the end of her career's upward path.

In the front row Poppy and her mother were horrified. All this talk of 'reporting the incident' was a pathetic code word for sending Poppy to jail. Mrs Pilot looked right at Poppy.

Poppy looked overwhelmed with fear but she did not bow her head. Such strength! Mrs Pilot marvelled at it. But then Mrs Pilot's concerns moved to herself. She tried to sound decisive, even though the decision was less than a minute old.

"Very well. I have heard the many concerns that have been raised tonight. I shall this evening contact London Police, and report what happened this afternoon as a teeking incident. After all, the safety of the children here is my highest priority, and cannot be compromised. I'm sure that the police will follow the appropriate path from there. Thank you for your attendance tonight. This meeting is now closed."

Her authority had been saved. Her position was secured. She congratulated herself on a job well done. Of course there was a price to pay, and she was content for Poppy to pay it.

She went back to her office, took off her shoes, put her feet up on her desk and dialled the number for London Police.

An hour later the police came to Poppy's house. A neighbour had put the two younger ones to bed during the meeting at school. Poppy and her mother knew that the police were coming, but that didn't make the shock of it any less. They were holding one another on the sofa when they first saw the flashing lights through their windows. It was a horrible sight. At least they didn't have the sirens on.

They were both crying as they heard the two officers saying something to each other outside. They heard the footsteps approach their door and then four heavy knocks. Poppy sobbed loudly. Miriam somehow found the strength to raise herself from the couch and answer the door.

Miriam Joshua had never known pain like this. She cried and wailed as her daughter was taken away. Poppy matched her level of distress. After ten minutes of explaining, sobbing, wailing and a little bit of dragging the two police officers emerged from the house with Poppy. They put her in their car and drove away, headed for the cells under the Charlton Courthouse.

Miriam collapsed on her floor, her heart broken.

Chapter Ten

Joanna

The prison guard didn't care. He had been in the job for over 20 years now. Never in his wildest dreams did he imagine that he would be putting children behind bars. But then teeking arrived and, well, in his opinion it was needed. The rules are the rules. If you don't want to go to prison, then don't break the rules. It was as simple as that.

Of course if everyone simply did what they should he would be out of a job and the prison would be empty. But he didn't feel there was much risk of that happening anytime soon. So he turned up for another shift, and he really didn't care who it was that he was looking after.

Tonight things were busy. The prison was overcrowded. The cells were meant to hold two each, but most were holding four. They had two beds against each wall - an upper and a lower bunk. There was a toilet in the back of the cell, with no screen or door for privacy. It smelt bad. No one cared. The 'girls under sixteen section' was a good shift to get.

They didn't fight, they didn't yell or swear at you like the men sometimes would. Mostly they just stayed in their cells and cried.

The guard wasn't happy to have the police deliver him another prisoner. He told Poppy to go into a room to get changed. He gave her a dull green coloured jumpsuit and a garbage bag. The guard barked some instructions at Poppy: "Right - you've got two minutes to get out of what you're wearing and into this. Put everything you are carrying into this bag and you'll get it all back when you leave. Might be tomorrow, might be never. Hurry up."

Poppy hurriedly got into the awful uniform. Her hands were trembling as she got changed. She finished and came out of the little changing room.

The guard saw her. "Leave the bag on that seat there and I'll process it. Come with me." As the guard took Poppy to her cell, he didn't even notice that she was crying. They all cried, except the Australian who had been brought in a few hours earlier. She was unusual. But right now, he took Poppy to her cell as if locking up 14 year old girls was the most normal thing in the world.

Poppy herself was fighting back fear, revulsion and disgust all at once. But mostly fear. All of this might have been normal to the guard but it wasn't to Poppy. She was just 14 years old, and now she was spending her first night in prison. The guard stopped at a cell. He fumbled with his keys. He opened the door. "Go in there", he said to Poppy with an expressionless voice. "Lights go out at 10:30 - in half an hour."

At this point he often had to drag them in, because many would collapse on the floor in distress.

However Poppy walked into the cell. He closed the door behind her and fumbled with his keys once more. With a click the door was locked. The guard walked back down the corridor, and Poppy was all of a sudden the furthest thing from his mind.

Poppy stood near the cell door, staring at three faces, which were each staring back at her. To Poppy's left sitting on the bottom bunk was a girl who looked a year or two younger than her. Her eyes were full of fear and her cheeks were covered in tears. She didn't say anything.

The bed above her was empty, so Poppy assumed that was where she would be sleeping. To her right, on the lower bunk, was a girl about Poppy's age. She had the same long face and tear-stained cheeks as the first girl. She also didn't say anything for now. Poppy would have looked at her longer, but because she had glanced up, she was unable to glance back down. Sitting on the top bunk to her right Poppy was stunned by the face that looked back at her. It was the last thing that she expected to see.

The girl didn't look afraid. She didn't look happy, but she wasn't as distraught as the other two obviously were. She said, "Hi." Her face and voice betrayed no fear. She was just happy to see someone new. She was dark-skinned. There was nothing surprising about that - many Londoners had African ancestry. But her features were not what Poppy was expecting. The shape of her face and the way her hair fell made the girl unlike anyone Poppy had seen before. Well, she was unlike anyone Poppy had ever seen before - in person.

She had seen pictures and videos of people who looked like this girl. And the most famous of all of the people who looked like this was Danielle Tunupingu.

Poppy was so surprised and intrigued by the dark-skinned girl on the top bunk that she almost forgot how afraid she was. Poppy climbed up to her bunk and looked across the small cell at the girl. "What's you name?" Poppy asked. The girl answered, "I'm Joanna. I'm not from here. I'm from Australia. Who are you?"

"My name's Poppy. I'm, well, I live here, in London. You look a bit like Danielle you know."

"Ha! You know my cuz! Everyone knows her."

"Your what?"

"My cuz. My cousin. She's famous, she is."

"Your cousin! Danielle Tunupingu is your cousin! That's amazing! But what are you doing here?"

"Well, we are visiting England. To meet some people. It's not going well. I didn't want to come to this place. But I'll be going back home soon."

"So who are you with?"

And that was all the invitation that Joanna needed.

She began a long and detailed account of her extended family, about where everyone fits in the family tree, and how many of them had come on this trip to Britain (about a dozen). She told of where Danielle was from (down the road from Joanna), she spoke of how she was looking forward to being home, as that's really the only place that she ever really wants to be.

Poppy was both fascinated by this conversation, but at the same time she was all too aware that she was in prison.

She wanted to know a hundred things about the prison and what she was doing here, but Joanna was simply too interesting to allow any conversation about all that. It would have to wait.

Poppy interrupted Joanna's long description of her family. "But I don't understand why you are here. Like, what exactly are you doing?"

Joanna replied, "Well, Danni got asked to do some interview. So they paid for us. But Danni thinks there are some people here that might know where this might all go."

"I don't get it - what do you mean where this might all go?"

"Teeking, you call it. Where it might go. What might come along as well."

"You mean... there might be other kinds of teeking or something?"

"Yep. We have stories about that. But what you done?"

"Oh right." Poppy had been engrossed in these stories from Australia, of people so different and so far away.
But with that simple question Poppy's mind came racing back to her own depressing circumstances. "Well, it's been a very good day that has turned into a very bad day for me." And with that Poppy then started to explain everything that had happened. It was only some nine hours ago that she was sitting next to Elz in the sunshine. But it felt like an age ago - so much had happened. She actually found it quite a release

to explain it all, to go through it piece by piece, and reflect on what had occurred. Once she had given her story right up to her arrest and coming to the prison, she stopped.

Joanna said, "My people have stories of things like that you know."

Poppy was stunned. She had no idea what had happened to her in the classroom earlier today.

She could barely explain it to anyone. No one knew what to make of it, most of all herself. But here was a young girl, a complete stranger from the other side of the world, hearing the story and thinking that she knew what was going on.

Poppy said, "Things like what?"

"Like what you just said - people getting better when they are sick. Power coming out and changing things. That stuff. Those are not new to us."

"So you think what happened to me today has happened to people before?"

"Yep. I reckon it has."

"No way!"

"Yeah - it has!" Joanna laughed. She had been handed down her people's stories her whole life. They were not new to her - they were all she had ever known. To meet someone to whom they were so foreign was unusual.

"Then, if that's true," Poppy said, "then there are people who know what happened today, people who can explain it."

"For sure Poppy" Joanna replied. Joanna looked at her and realised that she knew so little - she seemed so lost about what she had the power to do. So Joanna started talking. She told how her people had lived in certain parts of Australia since before anyone could remember. She talked about the macadamia trees, and the nuts that they produced, and the ways in which her people ate them.

She explained the different stories that had arisen about things that had happened. Moving things around with your mind was just one story amongst many. But the point of doing special things was never just for amusement or for fun - there was always a reason, always a need for an action to be undertaken.

Poppy didn't understand the stories - they sounded like fairy stories except with lots of strange animals instead of Humpty Dumpty and Cinderella.

But they all involved people doing things that sounded unrealistic - magical even. Ten years ago everyone, even people's Poppy's age and younger, would have dismissed the stories as myths. But teeking changed everything. This side of Danielle's breakthrough, no one was quite so certain of things anymore.

Poppy tried to put her thoughts together. As her mind was racing she slowly said to Joanna, "So it sounds like you are saying that teeking is just one thing that the nuts can make you do. There might be others."

Joanna laughed again. She had known it all her life. But it was fun seeing someone else catch on for the first time.

Poppy said, "Wow, I'm going to have to think about that." Without doing it deliberately, Poppy lay down in her bed and wondered what power she might have discovered.

After a few minutes of pondering she realised all of a sudden that she had never asked Joanna what had caused her to be thrown in jail. In an hour's conversation it hadn't come up once. "Joanna! I didn't ask - sorry! But what happened to you today that they put you in here?"

"So Poppy, I've been experimenting with this."

"With what?"

"Some people don't like it, which is why I'm in trouble. Are you ready?"

"Ready for what?"

"Don't freak out."

"Why would I freak - "

At that moment Joanna looked at Poppy. The lights had gone out in the cells some time ago, but there was enough street light coming in the windows and from the green exit signs around the corridors so that they could see one another easily.

Poppy was lying on her bed, looking up at the roof.

The blank roof was the main thing in Poppy's vision.

But as Poppy looked at the roof, words appeared in her mind. Each word flashed before her in large red capital letters for a split second.

Four words came and went in not much more than a second. The words were:

I

CAN

DO

THIS

Poppy screamed. You would think she had seen a spider the size of a plate such was the sound her lungs produced. All hell broke loose - some of the girls in the nearby cells shouted out, wanting to know what had happened. The two girls in the bunks below them got up and were looking around to see what the matter was. It seemed like 20 different people were all speaking at once.

Poppy then shouted out, "What was that? What on earth was that?" The guard heard the commotion but was too lazy to get out of his seat. He simply yelled down the corridor at the top of his voice, "Quiet!" Like so many parents before him he didn't even realise that he was contradicting himself.

The only sound that was out of place was the sound of Joanna laughing. For a full minute she had people all around her demanding to know what had happened, yet she laughed and laughed to herself.

Poppy had flown out of the bed and was standing on the cell floor looking like she was ready to tackle someone. Joanna interrupted her own laughter to say, "I told you not to freak out!"

"Far out Joanna. I wasn't expecting that. It scared me!" As Poppy got her breath back she started to see the funny side of it. A smile crept up the sides of her mouth as she realised all the commotion that she had caused. She looked at Joanna. "So that's what you can do is it? Yeah, I can see why that would get you into some trouble." Poppy climbed back up to her bed.

An hour later Poppy lay on the bed, wide awake. This had been the worst day and yet she struggled to feel bad. Her mind raced with thoughts about Elz, of how she felt in that moment at school, of Joanna and the red letters that she had made appear in her mind. It was a day unlike any other that she had ever known. Her thoughts would sometimes veer towards being in Mrs Pilot's office, of the horrible meeting at school, of the police coming to her home, and of the awful place she was lying in right now. But she would push these out of her mind and go back to the sunlight that drenched them as they did their schoolwork, the look on Elz's face and the strange new friend who seemed to know so much lying across the cell from her. How could one day fit so much good and so much evil into it?

She didn't care to imagine what tomorrow might hold.

Chapter Eleven

Mrs Browning

On Friday morning Poppy woke up feeling exhausted. She had not slept well at all.

She had an uncomfortable bed, unfamiliar surroundings, too much light from other parts of the prison and noise from the other girls, the guards and the traffic outside. But most of all she had fear. That disturbed her far more than everything else put together.

There was banging and crashing of doors further down the corridor. The day had started, not that any of the girls inside the cell knew what a prison day involved. A guard was talking and there were others voices echoing around the concrete corridors as well.

Joanna was already awake. She was sitting up on her bed with her arms around her legs. She looked like she had seen enough of England and was ready for home. Joanna was looking out of the window, not that there was anything worth looking at - just the building across the road. It was raining heavily outside.

Poppy said, "Hi."

Joanna spun and smiled. She was obviously glad to have some company. "Hi Poppy. You OK?"

Poppy paused. "No. Not really. I'm ... well, I'm scared. I don't want to be here."

"None of us do."

The girls sat in silence for a while. The noises coming down the corridor were getting closer.

A few minutes later a guard came to their door and unlocked it. It was a new guard - not the one that had been on duty last night. Even though he was at the start of his shift, he used a tired voice to speak to them. "Listen up. Right, here's your breakfast. In an hour or so you'll have a visit from Mrs Browning, the prison lawyer. She's going to give you some advice because you'll have bail hearings later in the day."

Four trays with food on them were given to the four prisoners. It was a plate covered by a scalding hot pile of yellow goop. Poppy wasn't sure if it was scrambled eggs disguised as vomit, or vomit disguised as scrambled eggs. Either way she wasn't particularly hungry and there was no way that she would be eating it.

Two pieces of cold toast were on the side of the plate, looking like they were trying to escape from the pile of yellow goop. Vainly they pushed towards the edge of the plate but alas, the goop was too strong. It had begun to cover them and any dream of escape was crushed under the steaming pile of yellow awfulness. Poppy broke off a piece of the toast that had thus far avoided the goop and chewed it. It was bad.

An hour passed in which nothing much happened.

Another guard collected the four barely-touched breakfasts and took them away. Then the guard came back.

He unlocked the door and without stepping into the cell said in a bored voice, "Mrs Browning will now talk to you about the hearings later on." A lady shuffled into the cell behind him, and was looking through a big folder full of papers.

Julia Browning had been a lawyer for over 25 years. But it looked as though that was 20 too many. She wore a plain pair of black pants, and a pleasant enough orange, brown and yellow knitted jumper. Her hair was short and curly. It was styled for ease of management, not for looks. But it was more what she wasn't wearing - there was no effort, no make-up, no smile, no energy.

Once upon a time it had been an adventure for her, a mission to learn how things work and then a way to set the world to rights. Once upon a time she had bounded into lectures, bounded into her first job as a lawyer, bounded into helping clients who needed her to save them from prison.

As a young woman she attacked life with enthusiasm. But that was a long time ago. Over the years life had attacked her back. When she was 20, she thought that the sky was the limit. Now that she was 50, the credit card company determined what was the limit. She juggled her eldest daughter's unexpected pregnancy, the quest for an affordable house in London, her husband's computer game addiction, her elderly father's fight for life, and broken relationships with various family members and former friends. With all of those balls in the air she had no time or emotional energy left to bring to her work.

When she was a young lawyer, she had started an arm wrestle with the system. The system had won. She had taken on injustice, she was fighting for what was right, she was the one to bring truth. But she had been snowed under by delays, judges making crazy decisions, further delays, clients doing stupid things, more delays, workloads that were way too demanding, unnecessary delays, paperwork that defied logic, and delays so lengthy that they made the system achieve the opposite of what it was meant to do.

However that was all many years ago. Today it was simply about getting in and getting out, it was about doing the bare minimum and then she would be out of there, and free to keep juggling all of those balls for another day.

She gave the briefest of glances up from her papers and said to the four of them, "OK, so because there are so many in the prison, I've got just five or ten minutes with the four of you, so I will go through your cases one by one. Let's see, do I have Joanna T... tun... ooo... peen..."

"Tunupingu" Joanna said, putting the poor lawyer out of her misery.

"Yes. That's you is it, Joanna? Right. Let's see... oh right ... foreign national... arrested for uncertain teek crimes... hmmm a bit mysterious..."

The lawyer finally looked up from her notes and looked at Joanna. "So in cases where someone has come into the country and been arrested, they are usually sent home.

Now I see you've only been in the UK a short time. Do you have a flight home booked already?"

"Yes" Joanna answered. "I'm going home Thursday next week."

"Right, good" the lawyer replied. "Well today is Friday so if you tell the judge that you have a flight home booked for six days' time, then they will almost certainly release you on bail, and you will have to make sure you are on that flight. And that will be the end of that."

Without waiting for Joanna's reply the lawyer moved on. "Now do we have a Poppy Joshua?"

"That's me" Poppy said.

"Right. Now Poppy I see we have… oh right… allegations of inside teeking… well that's quite serious. So you are 14 years old… victim is in hospital…"

"Victim?" Poppy said loudly. "There's no victim! My friend got better!"

"Oh yes dear, but he's in hospital it says here. Look darling, let me explain how it works. Under the teeking laws, once someone has been through 24 hours in prison they are brought before a judge. At this point the police tell the judge what the person is accused of doing. The police will say if they want them to be put on trial at some point in the future, and if they do then there is a discussion regarding whether the person will stay in jail until the trial, or if they will be let out on bail. Bail means that the person is released, but they promise to turn up to their trial, whenever that happens to be. Are you following?"

"Yes" Poppy replied.

"The more serious a case is, the less likely the prisoner is to be granted bail. If someone has been arrested for five murders, then there is almost zero chance they will be released on bail. If someone teek-stole a mobile phone, then they will almost certainly be granted bail. And in between those two extremes there are cases where it could go either way."

"With teek crimes being out of control, there are long waits for matters to go to trial. So between the crime occurring there is often a full year before the trial can be held.

Now with young people the courts don't like to keep them in jail for a full year or any lengthy period, but they are getting more and more fed up with teek crimes. The judge will probably want to grant bail in your case. So Poppy, the best thing to do is just admit that you did the wrong thing, say that you are sorry and then you'll get bail, and you'll have a year or so to get ready for your trial."

"But I haven't done the wrong thing."

"Ah yes, I often get this. Human pride! It keeps me in business, it really does."

Poppy's tone of voice hardened. "I'm not being proud - it's the truth."

"Poppy you don't want to be in prison for the next year do you love? Did you imagine your 15th birthday behind bars, hmmm? And then if you are found guilty, they'll throw another 20 on top of that.

Do you want to go from being happy at school one day, to being stuck in jail until age 35? No you don't. So be smart - say you did the wrong thing and take it from there."

The lawyer wasn't interested in further conversation. She moved on to the girls on the lower bunks, giving Poppy no chance to say anything more.

Poppy's mind was reeling. A year! And then who knows what? It couldn't happen. It mustn't happen. She started to cry. She laid down on the bed and simply tried to block out everything around her.

She didn't know what to do. Her tears flowed freely into the horrible prison pillow.

A few minutes later the lawyer left the cell. The girls were silent, as they digested the lawyer's words to each of them. The noise of the banging and crashing of various prison doors had almost become so frequent that they ignored it.

The rain still fell heavily outside. It provided a background noise to everything else going on.

Joanna broke the silence. "Poppy."

Poppy was glad that Joanna had reached out. Poppy sat up and looked across the cell to Joanna. Joanna asked, "Watcha gonna do?"

"I don't know."

As the lawyer had explained it, she had to say that she'd done the wrong thing. All that Poppy knew was that she was sitting in class and she had been overwhelmed with kindness and love for her friend.

There had been power flow from her, and Elz seemed to be completely better as a result. What was wrong with that? Surely that was the most right thing that she had ever done in her life. How could she call that bad?

Poppy hated lying. She knew that other people could do it and not care, but she couldn't. She didn't know why she had such a strong dislike of it - it wasn't because any particular adult had drummed into her that it was bad. She just hated it and always had. She knew that when she lied, it made her feel as though she had swallowed poison.

It wasn't anything to do with getting caught for the lie, or the bad consequences that might follow. She was smart enough to be fully aware that there are many occasions where the person who lies gets away with it. Sometimes someone is better off for having told the lie. But for Poppy it was internal - once you have swallowed poison you are at risk. You have been made sick. At that moment it is all about what is inside you - it's not about other people at all. Of course some poisons the body can expel in a few hours. Others will ruin you for years. Poppy regarded lying as poison for the soul - a destroyer of what is right on the inside of a person, and something so harmful that it takes years to internally recover from.

Poppy could remember the day that she decided that she would never lie. She was 11 and she had seen another student get caught by a teacher for fighting in the playground. As she watched, the boy came out with a whole string of excuses, each one obviously a lie. Poppy felt disgusted that he could do it to himself - that he would diminish his own character so quickly and carelessly, as if it meant nothing at all. It almost made Poppy vomit. Her reaction was so strong that she resolved that she would always tell the truth, at whatever cost, no exceptions. So she did.

But now she found herself in prison, and a lawyer was telling her that a simple little lie would see her released later today. Telling the truth could ruin her life.

After a long pause Poppy said to Joanna, "What should I do?"

Joanna looked at Poppy. She stared at Poppy. She didn't say anything but it was obvious that an answer was coming. The pause didn't feel awkward even though it was lengthy. Poppy realised that at this moment Joanna had more than just the wisdom of a young girl a long way from home.

Joanna had a whole culture to draw down on, a whole history that she had consumed and understood. This gave her wisdom far beyond her few years of experience.

Joanna said, "Poppy, why did this happen to you?"

"I don't know!" Poppy shot back without thinking it through.

"Poppy, teeking is something that all people can do with a few nuts inside them. But how many people do you know who can do what you did yesterday?"

"Well I don't know anyone who's done it."

"Exactly. Because it came out of you. The nuts work with who you are to make the power come out. What you had inside you was so pure, and when that is joined with what the nuts contain, then it works together, like a man and a woman making a baby."

"Eww!"

Joanna didn't understand why Poppy gave that reaction.

Poppy realised she was being childish, and quickly considered what Joanna had just said. Poppy asked, "Do you think that other people can do what I did?"

"I don't know. But what happened to you happened because of who you are."

"But why me?"

"I don't know - there is no way of knowing. But the nuts don't just give the same abilities to everyone. Those with the character to take action can do things that others can't. It sounds to me like you have the ability to make sick people get better. You've done it once. Imagine what you might be able to do in the future if you were trying. You are right at the start of finding out what you can do."

Poppy grappled with all this new information. "But I mean, you are making the nuts sound like they are alive. They sound a bit like Santa Claus - that they know who's naughty and who's nice. They are just nuts. They don't know things."

Joanna looked at Poppy, and raised both her eyebrows. She didn't say anything. She didn't need to. On the receiving end of that look Poppy realised that telling the cousin of Danielle Tunupingu what macadamia nuts can and can't do was a really bad idea.

Poppy retreated - "Well maybe they are something like that, I mean, I don't know all that much."

Joanna continued, "Poppy, if you are going to grow in what you can do, you need to develop on the inside, not just in teek skills as you say. If you change who you are, you won't be able to do it anymore."

Those words went straight to Poppy's heart. She knew it was true. Her character was the asset that she had to preserve. Nothing could destroy it. She knew that Elz was healed of cancer because of her.

She didn't plan to do it, she didn't ever imagine she could do anything like it. But she knew that she had done it, and she could very well do it to other people as well. If she could explain what had happened to her, perhaps she could even teach and train others to do it as well. That could lead to amazing places.

But lying would ruin it all. Poppy knew in her heart that this was a huge test, and if she failed it would change her character in a major way. What she had spent years building would crumble. There would be no bright future, nothing other than the memory of a beautiful moment and then a failure that meant her whole life would be spent reflecting on the fact that she morally peaked at age 14. She might skip out of prison today but all the decades to come would be spent in regret.

After a long pause Poppy said, "I'm telling the truth. It's the right thing to do. Others might not do what is right, but I do. It's why I was able to help Elz. It is who I am. If I stop telling the truth I won't be able to help anyone else."

Joanna nodded. "Yes - that's right. But understand Poppy that things happen for a reason. What happened yesterday is not just luck. It is the right time for this to be known. So if you think things are going bad, a way will be found. This is bigger than just you."

Poppy wasn't really listening anymore. She had made up her mind. She began to think it through. She was mentally building up the strength to stick to the plan, whatever it might cost.

Chapter Twelve

Judge Adams

The courtroom opened at 9am. But from 8:30am onwards there were large crowds of people outside the building. The teek courts were the most overused and under-resourced in the whole country. Every day there were lines of lawyers, staff members, defendants, witnesses, family members and supporters, who between them threatened to swamp the building like survivors clinging to a capsized ship.

Making his way through the staff entry, Judge Adams braced himself for the last day of the week. He liked teeking.

It had been good for his career as well. At a time when the nation needed new judges for all these teek crimes, he had been able to step into the role. Once he got there, he found that being a judge was the best job in the world. He loved the pomp and fancy ceremony, the judge's robes and the fact that the whole courtroom had to bow to him. It wasn't easy, however. The teek courts were extremely unruly. This was probably because the penalties were so severe, and many of the guilty were so young. To help the judges keep their courtrooms under control they had imported that beautiful bonus of life as an American judge - the gavel. 'Gavel' is the proper name for the little wooden hammer that judges get to bang at whatever time they feel like underlining what they have just said.

At first, Judge Adams had frowned and poured scorn on the need to import this Americanism into British courts.

In fact, there seemed to be an unofficial competition between all the judges to be the most displeased about gavels being introduced to Britain.

But then his gavel arrived. It was new, polished and gorgeous. It sat there on the bench and looked at him. It spoke to him of order, authority and power. Of *his* authority and power. Judge Adams resisted its flattery for barely five minutes. After the first morning Judge Adams adored his gavel and used it often. He banged it down with great enthusiasm whenever it was needed, and often when it wasn't.

Its sound was music to Judge Adam's ears. Of course he never did get around to telling the other judges that he had changed his mind about gavels. And they never got around to telling him the same thing as well.

Judge Adams wasn't a particular harsh or a particularly lenient judge. He just got on with the job of applying the teek laws as they stood. In his mind the law was there to keep people safe. It was all pretty simple to him - if you want to stay out of trouble then don't break the law. He had little sympathy for lawbreakers. It was like people who were caught speeding and complained about it.

They were surely the silliest people in the world. If you don't want a speeding ticket, then slow down. No one is stopping you. No one is pushing your foot down to make you go fast. He viewed people who committed teek crimes exactly the same way. No one makes you teek. If you don't want to go to jail, then don't commit teek crimes. It's that simple. He didn't care about the young age of many of the people punished for teek crimes. The law is what the law is. He had been a teenager once, and he knew that teenagers could tell right from wrong. It's just the law. If you don't like it, then start a campaign to have the law changed. Or move to another country where the law is different. Whatever. Just don't complain about your punishment if you break the law.

So Judge Adams had seen it all in his years as a judge. The crying, sobbing and shrieking. The yelling, raging and whinging. The distress, the agony and the pain. He didn't care. Those things were just the consequences of people's choices. If they made poor choices, they had to live with the consequences. That's how life is.

Judge Adams was happy with his choices. He was particularly happy with the bottle of wine he had selected to drink tonight. And on this rainy Friday his only ambition was to get through everything swiftly and get home at a reasonable hour. He had been assigned bail applications in Court One.

The downside of this was that Court One was busy, and that there was always a large number of bail applications.

The upside was that it was the biggest court room in the building, and the sound of his voice and gavel travelled beautifully through the whole room.

—

Poppy's prison cell was down in the basement of the court building. As the morning wore on Poppy noticed that people were being taken up towards the courtrooms, and they weren't coming back. There was a steady flow of girls from other cells going along the corridor past Poppy's cell to the right. Poppy and the other girls in her cell watched each one walk past.

Every few minutes the guards marched a girl past. All of them looked fearful and daunted by what lay ahead.

The horrible green uniform swallowed any of the girls' natural beauty or warmth. Then some minutes later the guards would return on their own, walking to the left. But then the pattern was broken.

To their right, where the exit was, a scream rang out. Someone was screaming as if they had been shot. Her cries silenced everyone else in the prison. It was a constant, repeated, full-volume scream. There was no pause, no let up and no change in the volume level. It was screaming like Poppy had never imagined that someone could scream.

It got closer. After a few more moments the guards came into view. They were carrying a girl who had been marched past an hour ago. Walking to the girl's left they carried her - she was fighting, wrestling, trying to break free, but the guards carried her back to her cell. As they opened the door they positioned themselves to push her inside.

Despite a final attempt to break free, she was thrown into the cell. The door was swiftly slammed shut and the screaming slowly turned into sobbing.

The two guards were exhausted. They took a few minutes in the corridor to catch their breath. The four girls in Poppy's cell were looking at them. One of the guards caught their eyes as he recovered from his efforts. After a few heavy breaths he said to them, "Hope you make bail, girls." He nodded in the direction of the girl they had just returned with. "She didn't."

Poppy started to panic. The full realisation that she might spend the next year in jail hit her like a train. She started to moan softly, not that she realised it. But before there was any chance to do anything, a different guard was standing in front of the cell. "Right, have we got Joanna Tunupingu?"

"Yes" Joanna replied.

"Come on then."

With that, Joanna was gone. Poppy was distraught to see her new-found friend leave. There was no chance for a proper good-bye or anything.

All of a sudden Poppy was without this girl who had helped her when she desperately needed it. Poppy stood at the front of the cell and yelled down the corridor, "Good luck Joanna!" But it was all too late. Joanna was gone and Poppy had no idea if she would ever see her again. However Poppy was certain that she didn't want to see Joanna come back to the cell in an hour or so.

The morning dragged on. Joanna didn't return. Poppy was lying face down on her bed. It looked like she was doing nothing, but on the inside battles were being fought. She didn't talk to the other two girls in the cell. A tray with some lunch on it was slid into the cell. An hour later it was untouched. It's not that Poppy wasn't hungry - she didn't even notice it.

Poppy's mind raced. If she told the truth, then there was no knowing what would happen. A year in jail was a genuine possibility. And after a year she could well be sentenced to 20 more. There was no doubt that she might be found guilty of some crime.

She didn't know what had happened to Elz yesterday - how could a court hope to understand it? Anything could happen.

Poppy mentally prepared to lose her bail application.

Firstly she mourned her family - her mother and her younger brother and her younger sister. She would hardly see them. She would not eat with them, holiday with them, laugh with them, celebrate birthdays with them or see her brother and sister grow up. Poppy cried huge tears into her pillow as she thought about how much she loved each of them. She wept and wept as she thought of how much it would hurt to be separated from them.

Then Poppy mourned her friends. She liked school. She liked being with the same fellow students each day. Of course some of them were annoying - some of the boys were silly, some of the girls were mean. But the thought of losing their company for at least a year was beyond awful. And within the school she had some great friends. There were friends that she had shared her deepest thoughts and fears with. There were friends she had laughed with, cried with, and whose company was a joy. To be ripped away from them was a dreadful prospect. She also thought of her cousins, her friends on her street, and all the various family friends that she would lose.

Their lives would carry on, but she would gradually slip out of their thoughts, and there was nothing Poppy could do about it. She shook with grief as she went through all the people that she might be taken away from.

Poppy mourned for her freedom. She faced the fact that she would not walk in a park, she would not jump on a train, she would not go to the shops, she would not walk out her front door and be free to go in whichever direction she wanted to. Her birthday would pass without a celebration, Easter, Christmas, and every day that was special would be taken away from her, ripped out of her life without her consent.

She sobbed and wept for all the choices that she would not get to make, and all the joy and goodness that she would be denied.

And then she cried for what was going to replace all of that. She cried for the fact that she would live behind bars.

She cried for the cruelty that she have to endure. She cried for the fact that every adult she would interact with would simply be doing their job. No one would care for her unless they got a pay cheque at the end of the week. There would be no beauty, no family, no freedom, just bars, wire, guards and pain that she would be stuck with, no matter how badly she wanted to be free.

Hour after hour Poppy cried into her pillow. She was in such great distress that her whole body was sweating even though it was cold in the cell. It was a tidal wave of emotion, the likes of which she had never known before. Hour after hour she cried until the pillow was soaked, not that she even noticed.

As the waves of sadness reached their most intense, the thought would pop into her head, "Don't tell the truth. Give them what they want and get out."

But every time the thought came, she knew that she wouldn't do it. At the back of her mind was the thought that if what Joanna said was true, then she might be able to heal many people with cancer.

But at the front of her mind was the knowledge that telling the truth was what she did. It was the right thing to do, and her deepest conviction was that by doing what is right, good things will result.

So the waves of grief continued to come. She was overwhelmed with sorrow. Poppy physically lay on her bed, but in her heart she resolved that her character would not falter.

At last Poppy stopped crying. She was determined and felt that she could move on. She raised her head and sat up. The two girls on the lower bunks were both gone. She had not even noticed them leave. She saw the tray of food. As soon as her eyes hit it she realised that she was hungry. After getting down from her bed she sat on one of the lower bunks and put the tray next to her.

She started to eat a sandwich, but just a minute later a guard appeared at the cell door. "Poppy Joshua?", Poppy nodded. She put the sandwich down and headed out of the cell and down the corridor. Judge Adams awaited.

Chapter Thirteen

Mr Starr

The stairs up to the courtroom were narrow. As soon as Poppy reached the top there were people everywhere. Guards and court staff were racing around. Two guards marched Poppy through the corridors. One of them called out to a staff member behind a desk:

"Glenn, I've got a Poppy Joshua."

The man at the desk quickly looked up, and looked directly at Poppy. "So you do, so you do. Court One, buddy." came the reply.

"Thank you."

Poppy was unsure why the man seemed so interested in her. He clearly looked closely, as if she was someone he had heard of before. The guards marched Poppy towards Court One.

They came to the Court One door and one of the guards unlocked it. They entered the courtroom into an area on the side of the court where there was a bench behind a railing. The guards motioned for Poppy to sit on the bench, where there were four other girls, all dressed in prison clothes. They all looked pale and terrified. Poppy assumed they were also applying for bail.

The courtroom was imposing. There was a big, fancy bench that towered high above the rest of the room, and Judge Adams was sitting in the centre of it, dressed in scary looking robes. It seemed to be designed to resemble a throne.

It almost would have made sense if there was a crown on the judge's head.

Instead the judge was wearing one of those strange wigs that judges wear. Anyone who tried walk down the street with something like that on would get laughed at. But since everyone in the courtroom seems to take the judge so seriously, he somehow managed to pull it off. When you have power then you almost have the ability to define what clothes are intimidating and what are ridiculous. And Judge Adams certainly had real power over Poppy and the four other girls who were in his courtroom this morning. Their fate was in his hands.

From his bench Judge Adams looked down on a long table, with a couple of police officers at one end. At the other end was a tall man wearing an obviously expensive suit and a nice watch. He had his hair slicked back and looked very relaxed. Then behind the table were rows of seating - about fifteen rows that were completely filled with people. There were also at least 20 people standing against the back wall, and in the aisles, and anywhere that they could find space.

The room was filled to bursting. Poppy had no idea why so many hundreds of people were there.

The thing that stood out about the people at the front of the room - the court staff, the judge, the police and especially the man in the suit, was that they looked, well, normal. It was just another day for them. There was nothing about what was happening that stressed them, or concerned them at all. They were just going through the motions of another day at work.

Poppy looked at the rows of people. After a short time she saw her mother sitting on the second row. Her heart leapt. She felt instantly overcome with emotion. She would have loved to leap over the rail in front of her and run to embrace her mother. She couldn't help but to begin to cry at the sight. Her mother did the same, and they stared at one another. Miriam was overcome with emotion as she saw her daughter. She would have been emotional anyway, but to see her own little 14-year-old girl in that green prison uniform was like a punch to her stomach. She reeled in pain and tears flowed down her cheeks.

Poppy hadn't actually sat down yet, so the guard nudged her and she sat. Poppy continued to scan the crowd.

Even though a police officer was standing and speaking to the judge, the crowd began to murmur and many of them were pointing at Poppy, and whispering to the person next to them. The noise level in the room rose noticeably. Judge Adams pretended to be annoyed, grabbed his gavel and banged it down, exclaiming, "Order!"

It slowly dawned on Poppy that all the murmuring in the room was because of her. People had heard of her and were interested to see her - not just her friends and supporters but pretty much everyone in the room. This was the last thing Poppy was expecting. Even the four other girls further up the bench were all looking down to Poppy.

Strangely, Poppy found this to be quite encouraging.

If she had done nothing unusual, if she had simply broken the teek laws in some minor way, then there wouldn't be all of this attention - she would be nothing special and her entrance into the courtroom would have gone unnoticed.

As she sat down she continued to look through the crowd. A number of her friends had taken time off school to be there. She made eye contact with each of them, and they gave her a small, discrete wave. She was thrilled to see that Michael, Max, Lloyd and Jake had all decided to come, and were sitting together in the front row, just as they had been at the meeting last night. As she had that thought, Poppy asked herself if that was right. Could the meeting at the school really have been last night? To her it had felt like a year had passed since those events. Surely that couldn't have just been last night? And yet it was.

The afternoon wore on. The four girls ahead of Poppy each had their bail applications granted. It turned out that the tall man at the other end of the table to the police officers was a lawyer who would act on behalf of each of the girls. He was winning for each of the girls he acted for. In fact it seemed to Poppy that this man was having more influence on what was happening than Judge Adams himself.

When he stood to speak to the judge, Poppy noticed that he was in fact even taller than what she had first thought. He was obviously talented at persuading people because every suggestion that he made the judge agreed with.

His suit, watch and haircut were just as persuasive as his words. The whole package was such that Judge Adams seemed incapable of resisting his charms.

As Poppy watched him go about his work as the four other girls were granted bail, she couldn't help but react to him. From somewhere deep inside herself Poppy disliked him.

She had disliked him from the instant she had looked at him. With every word that came out of his mouth she disliked him more. She couldn't fault what he said, she couldn't fault what he did, but for some reason her dislike of him just kept rising.

Finally, sometime after 2:00pm the case before Poppy was completed. The courtroom was still heaving with people.

Poppy noticed that Mrs Pilot had come into the room at some point, and was now sitting just behind the police officers. She had her head buried in some papers. She seemed to be working hard to ignore the hostile glances coming from the four boys in the front row.

A court staff member jumped to his feet and said in a loud voice, "The matter of Poppy Joshua."

The police and Judge Adams all moved paper around their desks. Judge Adams said to the lawyer, "Mr Starr do you act for Miss Joshua?"

The tall lawyer stood up and said, "Your Honour, I am available to act for Miss Joshua. However, I have not had the opportunity to talk to Miss Joshua as yet. Under regulation 14, I am entitled to talk to her for 40 minutes before the matter comes to the court."

Judge Adams was clearly unimpressed. He had progressed through the day's matters at a healthy speed. He was on track to be in front of his fireplace with a nice glass of wine in his hand possibly earlier than expected. He wasn't interested in delays.

"Yes, if you must. Forty minutes, and not a minute more. I note that on the previous occasions when this has been needed today the discussions have been very short.

Therefore I will not stand down but will remain here at the bench. You may proceed."

"Thank you, your Honour." The tall lawyer then looked at Poppy and motioned for her to come towards him.

The security guard obviously knew what was happening because he opened a gate in the railing and indicated for Poppy to step through and sit at the table with the lawyer. Judge Adams busied himself by playing with piles of paper, and everyone else in the court chatted amongst themselves.

The lawyer spoke to Poppy in a soft voice so that they could have some sort of privacy even though there were hundreds of people in the room waiting for them to finish.

"Poppy, I'm Mr Starr, a lawyer appointed to represent you. Earlier today you probably spoke to one of the other prison lawyers, Mrs Browning. I work with her and my role is to do the talking before the judge on behalf of those seeking bail. What we want to do right here is get you bail and then worry about everything else later on. If you will -"

Poppy interrupted him - "I didn't appoint you."

The lawyer was taken aback at being challenged. "No, you didn't. The court did. For your benefit. You don't have to do what I say, you don't have to let me act for you, but everyone does.

Now, all you have to do to get off is say that you didn't mean to teek, and that you are very sorry that you did it, and that you definitely won't do it again."

"I'm not sorry I did it."

"Oh" said the lawyer. His eyebrows shot up his forehead as his face showed surprise. "Well, you have to say that you are. I'm sure that you are - you're a good kid. I will say those things on your behalf, and there should be no problem getting bail.

That's the stuff that the judge wants to hear."

"I told you I'm not sorry, and I'm actually quite open to the possibility of doing it again."

"Oh" said the lawyer, once more. His eyebrows were further up his forehead this time. He paused for thought. This was not how it normally went for him in these situations. He frowned and said, "Right, yes.

Well look, you realise that if you don't get bail you will spend from today until your trial - which could be over a year away - in jail? I'm sure that when you realise that you will be happy to let me say all the things that need to be said.

Frankly, your life depends on me saying these things.

Poppy this is what I do, and I'm good at it. This is my bread and butter. I got all those other girls out on bail, and I'll get you out too."

"I won't have you lie for me. I don't lie, I hate lies, so don't do it. I don't care if it's your bread and butter. I don't live by bread alone."

"Whatever - forget the bread thing. Poppy it's just a little white lie, but it will save you from an entire year in prison for goodness sake! You have to understand that in here, this is how the game is played.

Everyone knows that you may or may not actually be sorry, everyone knows that you will likely teek every day between now and your trial. But in this room we all put on a bit of a front and say what needs to be said. That's the system.

Everyone plays the system. There's no shame in doing it - everyone's doing it. You would be mad to not do whatever it takes."

"I'm not doing it, and you're not doing for me. Forget it."

"You can't be serious Poppy!" The lawyer noticed that Poppy did indeed look very serious. He looked around as his mind raced to come up with a plan B. He said, "OK. Well I guess what you should do then is simply throw yourself at the judge's mercy.

Whilst I'm talking I want you to cry a lot, be obviously distressed. I will say that you don't know what happened, that you are so sorry that someone was hurt -"

"No one was hurt. My friend got healed of cancer. I'm not sorry about that. In fact I'm thrilled."

The lawyer was stunned. He eyebrows had possibly never been this far up his forehead before.

He had never met a child who knew their own mind like this. "Well that's what you think might have happened, but that's not going to be believed.

I mean, really? Cancer? Sure, whatever. But the point is to get bail we need to show that you are afraid, sad, desperate, confused, all of that. That it was all an accident, and even then it might not work. My perfect record might not survive this madness. Can you do that?"

"So you want me to, like, put on an act?"

"Call it whatever you like, but that's what I want you to do. Cry, be sorry, let me say that you are sorry. This is a high risk approach, but if we jump off the wall together, so to speak, we should land safely. Surely you can do that?"

"No."

"What!" The lawyer's response was so loud that many of the people nearby turned and looked at them.

"No, I am not going to let you give the judge a false impression of what I think. I'm not going to put this little experiment to the test. The answer is no."

The lawyer stared at Poppy with an open mouth. He had never had an adult say these things to him, much less a teenager. He considered for a moment if a plan C was somewhere in the back of his mind. He quickly realised that it wasn't. The foolishness of it all was overwhelming to him.

All that remained was what he called the 'shock and awe' option. He wound himself up and let fly:

"Listen to me Poppy. I have been a lawyer for a long time. I know what works in this place and what doesn't. I am what stands between you and you spending the next year of your life in jail. You want what I am offering. You want it more than you realise. I don't care for people who take a stand on principle.

Actually I despise principles. Having principles gets you thrown in jail. Don't you dare be so stupid. Look at your mother over there and for goodness sake do what I say.

Follow my lead and you will spend tonight in your mother's arms. If you reject me then you'll spend a year in jail, which frankly you'll deserve for being so damned idiotic. So kid, wise up and do what I say. Is that clear?"

Mr Starr's voice had been rising with each sentence, and half the courtroom could hear the end of his speech.

Heads turned everywhere and looked at him. Poppy didn't care. She looked at him straight in the eye. As his speech had gone on, she made up her mind. It ended up being quite easy.

"Get out", she said.

"What?"

"Get out of here. You will not speak for me. Leave."

The lawyer slumped back in his seat. So all his tactics had failed. He looked at Poppy with contempt, and shook his head. "Okay then. Have it your way."

Miriam Joshua had been watching the exchange closely. She strongly disliked the lawyer but she couldn't tell why. But then when he had been raising his voice, she felt a strong urge to protect her daughter. Poppy didn't need helping, but her mother didn't know that and wasn't taking any chances. She decided to make him regret talking to Poppy like that.

Miriam looked around for something that would teach him a lesson. On the big table where the police and lawyers sat, there were papers everywhere and some law books as well. She looked at the biggest, heaviest book on the table. It was huge, which made it perfect. She stared at it for two seconds and it began to move. The two police prosecutors were talking to themselves and didn't notice. The book rapidly accelerated as it flew through the air.

Miriam sent it with as much force as she could muster. Only at the last split second did the lawyer see it coming. There was nothing he could do. The book violently smashed into his head and sent him sprawling on the floor.

He cried out in pain and surprise. The half of the room that wasn't already looking in his direction did so now.

People jumped up to help him off the floor.

Poppy had no idea why a book had flown across the room into the lawyer's head. But she was happy that it did.

Once it struck him the book bounced off his head and landed on her leg, down near her heel. It actually hurt a bit - the book was heavy and the hardback corners were pointed. But she didn't have time to worry about it for long.

Judge Adams exploded into life. He leapt up from his seat and banged his gavel the hardest he had ever done. He screamed, "Order! Order! There is no teeking allowed in this courtroom!" His face was red with anger. He looked out at the packed room and knew that there was no way he would ever find the culprit. He glared at all of them. For the next five minutes he raged at them, denouncing whoever had done this in the strongest language he could come up with. Like water fleeing a burst dam, the words flew out of the judge as he let the room have it for this unexpected action.

"How dare someone commit this assault right here in this courtroom! In all my years I've never seen such outrageous actions in a court of law! The person who did this will hand themselves in to the police officers right here in front of me. What a vile, horrid thing to do to such a decent man going about his work. This is a scandal!"

Miriam sat there perfectly still. Her face betrayed nothing. No one would have thought it was her. Many thought that it was Michael, Max, Lloyd or Jake. As she sat through the speech, Miriam maintained her concerned look.

But on the inside, she was regretting nothing.

Once Mr Starr had been helped back to his feet, he went back to where his papers were on the table. The book had done no lasting damage - he would have nothing worse than some swelling and a headache to show for it. He sat at the lawyer's table as the tirade from the bench continued.

Once he had concluded his lecture, Judge Adams turned to look at Mr Starr.

"Mr Starr I am deeply sorry that you had to endure that attack. I've never known anything like that in this courtroom. However, it appears that you are able to continue. The matter at hand is the bail application of Miss Joshua. Can we continue with that?"

Looking like he needed a holiday, Mr Starr replied, "Your Honour, I have concluded my discussions with Miss Joshua. She does not wish for me to represent her in this hearing, so I will leave her to make her own application."

Judge Adams' eyes widened for a moment. "Oh! That is most unusual. Everyone else does what the lawyer says. In fact I've never seen this happen before. I mean, is there any possibility that she will change her mind?"

"Your Honour this is indeed an unusual child. Her mind is not for changing. I shall withdraw."

"Yes, thank you Mr Starr." The lawyer quickly bundled his papers up and left the courtroom. He didn't look at Poppy as he left. He didn't want to.

Chapter Fourteen

Miriam

Judge Adams looked at Poppy. "Now, Miss Joshua, since you have chosen to conduct your own application for bail I will explain to you what will happen. Firstly, you can remain at the table where you are currently seated.

Secondly, the police prosecutor will explain to the court why they have arrested you, and what charges are being laid against you. They will lead some evidence against you, and they will say if they support or oppose bail being granted.

Once they have finished doing this, then you can respond and say whatever you like. But you will be sworn in and what you say must be the truth. Your evidence can be used at the trial, whenever that might be. Do you understand?"

Poppy was about to answer, but the guard standing next to her nudged her and signalled to stand up. Poppy took the hint, and stood up. "I understand, your Honour."

"Right then," said Judge Adams, "Madam Prosecutor what is your position on this matter?"

The police prosecutor stood and said, "Your Honour under section 145 of the Teeking Act this is a school referral, so in a moment I will lead evidence from the relevant head teacher, Mrs Pilot of Charlton High School. The charges against Miss Joshua include inside teeking, and the law requires the police to oppose bail in all cases of inside teeking, so bail is therefore opposed."

"Yes, thank you. You can lead your evidence then."

The prosecutor then asked Mrs Pilot to stand in the witness box. Mrs Pilot promised to tell the truth, and then a load of rubbish came out of her mouth. She made out that she was the hero who was acting to protect the innocent little lambs who attend the school each day. They needed to be saved from the nasty, threatening 14-year-old girl who wanted to be a character from a horror movie and do evil teeking experiments on their insides. You could tell Judge Adams was turned off by it, which Poppy thought was a good thing. On the front row Michael, Max, Lloyd and Jake were so noticeably rolling their eyes and shaking their heads that Poppy was surprised Judge Adams didn't tell them to stop.

The prosecutor kept asking questions, which Mrs Pilot continued to turn into opportunities to describe her brilliance as a head teacher. Judge Adams then started asking questions to Mrs Pilot himself. He said, "Mrs Pilot, how was the young man, Eleazar, affected by what happened?"

Mrs Pilot replied, "Well, by the accounts of all the boys in the room he was doing things that he could never do before, it was like he was delirious, so clearly the incident had a big effect on him."

"Yes. And is there any doubt that it was Miss Joshua who was the one who caused this?"

"No, by her own account it was her... um... actions that changed his... mood, well, his health."

"Yes." Turning to look at the prosecutor, Judge Adams said, "Is there anything further you wish to ask Mrs Pilot?" Picking up the hint that the judge really didn't want to hear anything more from her, the prosecutor quickly replied, "No, your Honour."

Now Judge Adams turned to Poppy. "Miss Joshua, you will now be sworn in and you can lead any evidence you wish. Under section 145, to be granted bail you simply need to acknowledge that you did the wrong thing and commit to not doing it again. I would think that you would want to keep that at the top of your mind." He turned to one of the court staff and said, "Please swear Miss Joshua in."

A man that Poppy had barely noticed until now jumped up from a desk to the side of the judge and spoke loudly to Poppy. "Please stand, and take the bible, holding it up in your left hand and repeat after me."

The prison guard nudged Poppy again, so she stood up. She hadn't noticed a book in front of her, but the guard put it in her hand. Perfectly on cue, thunder sounded from the storm clouds outside.

Poppy looked at the man with the loud voice.

He said, "I swear by Almighty God."

Poppy felt a rush of blood to her head. She was overwhelmed by a sense that this was a critical test for her.

Hundreds of eyes looked at her across the room. She also had the sense that she had passed this test already - that she passed it on the prison bed earlier that morning. She spoke slowly and loudly, "I swear by Almighty God."

"that the evidence I shall give."

"that the evidence I shall give."

"shall be the truth."

"shall be the truth."

"the whole truth."

"the whole truth."

"and nothing but the truth."

"and nothing but the truth."

Judge Adams then spoke to Poppy, "Miss Joshua you should remain standing. This is your application for bail. You may say why you think you should be granted bail, but bear in mind what I said earlier about the things that you need to say - that you did the wrong thing and you won't do it again."

Poppy looked around the courtroom, and caught her mother's eye. She felt loved. She loved seeing the boys on the front row, and could feel their support. They would have tackled the prosecutor to the ground if she asked them to.

Saying the oath had put fresh wind in her sails. She felt fear and peace at the same time, which was a strange combination.

She refused to hide anything of what happened, or to mislead in any way.

She spoke in a voice that surprised people with its clarity and strength. "Your honour, I was in class yesterday and I was overcome with compassion for my friend, Eleazar, who has cancer. I don't really know what happened next. It has never happened before. Power went out from me. I didn't know that I had that power, but I did. The power went into Elz, and he was healed. He doesn't have cancer anymore.

That's what happened, so I should be let out of jail, because I didn't do anything wrong, I didn't do any inside teeking. In fact, something very wonderful happened, and everyone should be happy about it."

Judge Adams was not expecting this. He chuckled softly under his breath and said, "Well you say that he was healed of cancer. I doubt that very much."

Sitting on the front row Max was outraged by the judge's arrogant dismissal of what he had seen with his own eyes. He yelled out, "Well Elz says that he's healed, and he'd know better than you."

The whole room turned and looked at Max. Murmuring broke out everywhere. Judge Adams frowned severely and swiftly banged his gavel twice.

"Order! Order!" he shouted. "I will not have members of the public gallery interrupt these proceedings! Silence!"

With his face turning bright red very quickly, Judge Adams continued shouting, "Well at least this time we know who did it! The young man who just spoke out will not do so again. Security, remove the boy from the courtroom. I will not allow this hearing to turn into chaos with people shouting and speaking out of turn. I demand order!"

A number of security staff made their way towards Max. Without too much pushing and shoving Max left the courtroom, not before he loudly told the security men that Elz was actually healed, and that he saw it himself.

Once Max was out of the room Judge Adams turned back to Poppy, but he forgot to stop frowning. "Miss Joshua, so you admit it was you who teeked the boy, Eleazar?"

Poppy replied, "It was me that the power came out of. But I don't think it was teeking. I think the nuts can do other things that we haven't learnt about yet. I think this is the start - "

"Miss Joshua, you are accused of inside teeking. Your victim is in hospital. You admit it was you. That is all that the law requires. I have no interest in your speeches."

Poppy's shot back, "So it's against the law to heal someone from cancer?"

"No, of course it is not against the law to heal someone from cancer!"

"Then why am I in jail?"

A wave of murmurs spread over the courtroom. Obviously there was much agreement with the point that Poppy was making. On the front row the body language of Michael, Lloyd and Jake left no doubt that they thought Poppy had won that round.

Judge Adams tried to start his reply, but no words came out. He reached again for some words, and still his mind couldn't find any. Judge Adams could feel himself blushing. After an awkwardly long pause he said, "Look, under section 274 of the Teeking Act, any attempt to move things under a person's skin is classified as inside teeking and is a Grade 2 offence, punishable by up to 30 years imprisonment.

Frankly, I've been lawyer for over 30 years and I'm not really interested in a 14-year-old girl saying what is and isn't the law on teeking, as if all this education, learning and all the authority vested in the these courts by the state counts for nothing. It counts for a great deal I can assure you!"

Judge Adams knew that he was embarrassing himself but he didn't know how to stop. He didn't really know what it was about Poppy that enraged him so, but he knew that he really didn't like her. He continued, his voice creeping closer and closer to a shout:

"Now, Miss Joshua, it's almost 3pm. In a few minutes time I will send you back to jail where you will stay until your trial, which will be a year away if you are lucky. Granted the nonsense you have already spouted, you'll probably lose that trial and spend most of your life in jail. The only thing that can keep you from going back to jail at 3 o'clock is if you promise that you will not do it again. That's what this comes down to, so you had better give that assurance pretty clearly right now. What do you say?"

Poppy stared at the judge. In a soft tone she said, "If you were sick, if you had cancer, and you wanted me to, I would try to make you better."

The gallery loved it. There was a small outbreak of applause, and plenty of Poppy's supporters voiced their agreement.

Judge Adams slammed his gavel down repeatedly.

"Order! Order! Right, Miss Joshua, I will give you a final chance - will you promise to not do what you did again?"

Poppy just looked back at him. She had nothing more to say.

Judge Adams couldn't believe it. The veins on his neck looked like they might burst as his face went a further shade of red. "Ha! You'll say nothing then? So be it. Miss Joshua your application for bail is denied. Guards, you can return Miss Joshua to custody."

At that moment everything seemed to happen at once. Poppy's mother screamed, "No!" at the top of her lungs.

Poppy's other friends called out in the same vein.

Judge Adams furiously slammed his gavel down in an attempt to regain control of the room.

So hard did he belt it that it broke in two. The handle remain in his hand whilst the head bounced across the room. Poppy closed her eyes and slumped down in her chair.

The three boys were on their feet and moving towards Poppy. They were furious. Security staff were racing to cut them off.

Many other people were on their feet. Some of Poppy's other friends shouted out their objections. Judge Adams tried to drown out the noise by shouting, "Order! Order!" And at the same time there was a huge clap of thunder that made the whole courtroom shake, just to underline the drama happening inside.

Poppy felt crushed. She leant forward and buried her head in her hands. And yet she was not surprised. She was calm even though the courtroom was in chaos. The guard nudged her again. Poppy lifted her head up and opened her eyes. He told her to stand up. Poppy realised at that moment that she was not going to see her family and friends again.

She looked at her mum and blew her a kiss. And at that moment the emotion hit. Like a wave she was swamped - the tears began to flow.

But just as she thought she would be overwhelmed three words appeared in her mind, in large red capital letters:

IT

IS

FINISHED

Poppy instantly stopped crying. She ignored the guard who was trying to get her to co-operate in walking out of the courtroom. She scanned the room for Joanna Tunupingu. She hadn't seen her before now. Two guards had now started to push, pull and almost drag Poppy towards the door that she had come in. There was still bedlam all throughout the courtroom. Poppy's supporters were shouting at the judge. He was still shouting for people to be quiet, even though he was bereft without his gavel. Extra security staff had come bursting into the room and were looking for ways to throw their weight around.

Someone expressed their distress by teeking all of the police prosecutors papers in the air. Poppy was dragged by the two guards closer to the door. She was still twisting her head, looking for Joanna. Her heel was still sore from the book striking it, and she couldn't walk properly. Just as she was dragged through the door Poppy saw her - at the back of the room Joanna was looking right at Poppy. And then Poppy was gone.

The guards took Poppy back through the corridors and down the steps towards the cells. Poppy walked with them without complaining, even though she was limping because of her heel. The guards were unnerved by her calmness.

Numerous keys were put into numerous locks, and finally Poppy stood back in the corridor outside the same cell she had spent the night in. The guards unlocked the door, and motioned for her to step inside. Poppy felt calm. She had been tested. She had embraced the truth. She had sacrificed greatly for the sake of true character. She had done what was right, and on the inside she felt the satisfaction known only to those who walk with integrity.

Yet none of that diminished the horror of what stood before her. As the cell door swung open, the cell gaped its mouth wide, looking forward to consuming its prey. It had swallowed so many people before but it relished another victim. It didn't care about the pain. It didn't care about the suffering. It didn't care how much they cried.

All it ever wanted was one more. One more victim, one more prisoner, one more to hear the sound of the door shutting behind them. As the guards motioned for Poppy to step inside, the cell's hinges squeaked with joy. It loved this moment. It never got tired of a victim walking through the door. It relished the clang of the door closing behind the victim. That sound was the sweetest music it knew.

Poppy stepped into the cell. Squeak. Clang. It swallowed her whole.

She sat on one of the lower bunks. Joanna had said it is finished. Poppy didn't know why, but she felt that Joanna was right.

The guards locked the door behind her and walked back up the corridor. As soon as they were out of earshot one said to the other, "Wow, there's something different about that kid."

"Yeah, surely she is something special. I've never seen anything like that. Ever."

Chapter Fifteen

Elz

Elz was already a skinny kid. But then he got sick. He was one of those people with a big appetite who makes everyone wonder, "where does it all go?" But with Elz it was obvious where it went. He had a high-energy personality. He hated being still for any length of time. Not because he couldn't - anyone who had seen him on the video game console knew that he could. But because it was boring.

For Elz people were fascinating, life was fascinating, and every day was to be attacked with vigour rather than eased into. He didn't drink coffee, but it was as if he had been made with an internal supply that was turned on strong. For Elz life was too full of adventure to be worried about grooming, so he kept his blonde hair with a close crew cut. That way there was no hassle and no maintenance. It also meant that he wouldn't need to change anything if he one day joined the army.

So for those who knew him, the cancer was even more appalling for the fact that it left him tired, lethargic and glum. It robbed him of his personality as well as his health.

But now that was all in the past. Within an hour of the incident in room 29, Elz had been put in the back of an ambulance, and sent to hospital. But he wasn't happy about it.

From the minute that it happened, he knew in the depths of his heart that he was cancer free. He had been filled with life, with a fire that burned cancer away. He was healed, and he never doubted it. The only thing that puzzled him about it was that other people were not reacting with the same joy.

Yesterday he had been frail, sick and had no energy at all. Right now he felt fantastic. He was strong, he was bright-eyed and he was full of energy. This was obvious to everyone who had seen him before the incident. So why could people not simply be delighted for him?

He had no idea how Poppy had done it. But he didn't care. It worked, so who cares about anything else? If it's a mystery, then it's a mystery - but surely everyone can be happy about it! The first sign he got that people were not happy about it was within minutes of Mrs Greenwood rushing into the classroom. She had told him to sit down in his wheelchair. For the first time in months he had the energy to not just stand but to jump around!

As if he was going to sit down in his wheelchair! It was probably the silliest thing any teacher had ever said to him. So he ignored it. Instead he embraced Poppy and his friends. Deep down he knew that they had been a part of something special together, that they had witnessed an amazing event.

Half an hour later his mother arrived at the school, having been told to come in. He couldn't believe that his mother's reaction was to think that something had gone wrong. There he was - full of energy and smiling broadly, and his mother was worried! Could she not see that he looked better than he had for so many months? Elz knew that the cancer was terminal. He knew that he was dying, and that it would take his life. The treatment wasn't working.

The medical staff were trying their best but they were failing. The doctors and his parents tried to shield him from this reality. They went off and had long conversations without him in the room. But he was not stupid. His mum would come back from those talks with a tear-stained face and everyone looked very grim. What conclusions did they think he was drawing from all that?

Granted that was his situation, what could his mother possibly be worried about? What could be worse than dying? Yet when she looked upon his bright, healthy, vibrant face she started to worry!

Unbelievable!

But Elz knew that it was more panic than genuine worry. She just didn't know what had happened to her son.

She didn't know how she was meant to react. Because when they first locked eyes he saw utter astonishment on her face. Elz knew that within less than a second of seeing his face, his mother could discern that something had drastically changed for the better. Everything that had happened in the minutes since was just an act because his mother was so rattled she had no idea what to do.

If Mrs Greenwood and his mother were not crazy enough, once the ambulance arrived the medics were telling him to lie down on a stretcher so they could take him to hospital. The one place that he no longer needed to go was the one place that they were determined to take him. When they put his wheelchair near him to sit in he just teeked it away. Then he did the same with the trolley bed.

His mother had started yelling at him while they were still on the school premises. "Eleazar you get on the bed right now!" She was the only one who called him by his full name.

"I don't need it!", he yelled back.

"Until you've got a doctor telling you that you are better -"

"I am fine!"

The medics and the school staff didn't know for certain if he was better. But they could see that his lungs and voice were sure working well. There were a few more minutes of backwards and forwards between Elz and his mother, much of which was done at high volume. Finally Elz agreed to go in the ambulance if he could sit in the front. For the medics, that is not how it's normally done. But they thought it was likely the only way that they would get him into the ambulance at all. So they went with it.

Elz sat in the front and fumed that this was the celebration he was being forced to have. As the ambulance made its way to the hospital, he took his phone out of his pocket and made sure that everyone else knew what was going on. He opened his social media account and wrote "I feel awesome!!!!! Today at school Poppy teeked me free of cancer. I am 100% better. YES!!!!" and then hit 'post'.

They took Elz to the London Children's Cancer Hospital, which was where he had been receiving his treatment. The hospital's distinctive purple window stood out as they approached the entrance. When the hospital was built they asked some famous artists to design a coloured window.

The winning design was called *Purple Angels*. It was a collection of thousands of red, purple and blue angels that covered the entire eastern side of the building. It had won numerous awards and was the standout physical feature of the hospital. All patients and staff loved being on the side of the building that had the purple glass wall. But Elz had seen it so often that he barely noticed it as the ambulance got closer.

What Elz did see as they were stopped at a traffic light was food. There was a small grocery store that had various trays of fruit on the pavement. He felt a sudden wave of hunger sweep over him. He hadn't known hunger like this for so many months.

Elz lowered the ambulance window and teeked an apple into his hand. And a banana. And a few other things that looked good as well. He called out to his mum, who was in the back of the ambulance, "Mum you owe the fruit shop people some money."

"What? No I don't." She looked at him and saw him bite down on the apple. "Eleazar how dare you!" A minute later Elz was teeking a bank note through the air to a concerned looking shop keeper, who then smiled as he grabbed it. "Keep the change, buddy!" Elz shouted as the ambulance pulled away now that the traffic light was green.

The apple tasted beautiful. For at least the last six months he had been constantly urged to eat food that he didn't want to. He could hardly even remember what hunger was. But all of a sudden his taste buds were alive once more.

The apple was sweet, it was firm and it tasted better than any apple he had ever had before. Even the sound of each bite brought Elz a fresh wave of happiness. Elz attacked it as though there was a prize for demolishing it as fast as possible.

As soon as the ambulance arrived at the hospital, a staff member rushed up to the back of the ambulance with a wheelchair. He was a bit confused when a paramedic came out of the back. "Patient's in the front" the paramedic told the staff member.

But Elz was having none of it. He leaped out of the ambulance door and saw the man with the wheelchair coming towards him. "I'm OK" Elz said, and to make sure that the message was clear, he teeked the empty wheelchair out of the man's grasp and sent it speeding along the path at a considerable speed. "Hey!" the hospital worker said, and then teeked the wheelchair back to himself. But by then Elz was striding into the hospital entrance, with the rest of the group chasing after him.

He went straight to the reception desk. Looking the lady behind it straight in the eye, he said to her, "They want me to come in even though I'm totally better. It's crazy. So here I am." The receptionist looked at him with a blank expression. That is not how she is normally greeted. At first it was his words that confused her, but then she looked at him closer. "Is ... that ... you Elz?" Her eyes went wide as she realised it was him. He looked in perfect health, which was a massive contrast to when she had seen him last week. "Stagger me lad - you look great!" "I am great!" Elz replied, "Not that these clowns seem to realise it." He nodded his head in the direction of the group of adults who were chasing after him.

"Hey, you got any food there?" he asked the receptionist.

"No Elz, I don't have any food - does this look like the cafeteria?"

"Hmm, s'pose not." Elz replied.

The paramedics finally took Elz, who was cradling his collection of fruit in his arms, to a bed. As the afternoon went on and the rain fell outside Elz was put onto a ward and all sorts of observations were done. His mother stayed with him. Now that he was in the hospital she was more relaxed, and she began to enjoy his company, and he enjoyed hers.

She spent many months coming to grips with the fact that her son would die. She began to take the first steps of realising that he would not. She didn't dare admit to herself what was obvious - it had been a complete and instant healing, and he was now in perfect health.

A whole string of doctors and nurses made their way to his bedside with machines and clipboards containing notes - every conceivable shape of machine had been wheeled into his room at some point. Elz groaned every time a new machine was brought in. Could they not see that he was well?

Yet not a single doctor seemed to even take him seriously when he explained what had happened.

A senior doctor came in and said that they wanted to do some scans, and then keep him in overnight. In fact, he would remain in the hospital for several nights while they did all sorts of tests and got the results from every scan that they were going to do.

Elz roared his disapproval. "Days! You want to keep me in for days! No way! There's nothing wrong with me! Oh this is a joke." Elz underlined his point by teeking the clipboard in the doctor's hand and throwing it across the room. "Eleazar!" his mother shouted. The doctor was unhappy.

"Now young man, we want to be sure that nothing concerning happened to you today. In any case, there is a strict 'no teeking' policy within the hospital, so don't do that again."

Elz replied, "So if I start teeking stuff you'll kick me out? OK then - "

The blanket that was neatly folded on the end of the bed flew up into the air.

"No!" the doctor shot back, "we won't be kicking you out." The doctor took a step forward and grabbed the blanket out of the air. "We just expect you to behave better than you have been."

Elz looked at all the disapproving adult faces around him and decided to retreat into sullenness. "Whatever" he replied to the doctor.

He spent the rest of the afternoon and evening being tested for this or that - the whole procession of medical professionals poking and prodding his perfectly healthy body continued. He could hear whispers as the doctors seemed to slowly come around to the idea that he might be cancer free.

The doctors coming to see him were more and more senior, and the discussions amongst them were more and more lengthy. They kept asking him to explain again what had happened in room 29. He told the same story every time, but he could tell they didn't want to believe it. It was obvious that they thought that there was more to the story.

His mum decided that she would go home. They had run out of things to talk about. Finally Elz was left more or less alone from 8pm. He jumped onto his phone.

It's hard to say which gave him the biggest shock - the massive response to his earlier post or the fact that there was a whole school meeting happening right now. He stayed glued to his phone screen as various people gave updates during the meeting. It seemed ridiculous to him that he wasn't there. Surely what he had to say about what happened mattered more than anyone else? And yet there was an entire school hall full of people giving their opinion on what happened to him - with not a single one of them having spoken to him about it. Crazy.

Eventually, despite the hospital noise and lights, he managed to fall asleep.

-

The next day, Friday, Elz woke up feeling brilliant. Amidst all the drama with the hospital, every few seconds he realised how good he felt, and how long it had been since he felt like this. Breathing properly. His mind active. Full of energy. He looked at the particular blue angel that was staring down at him from the window. It was beautiful, but he just wished he could be on the other side of the glass.

Whilst it was absurd to him that he was in a hospital of all places, at least he knew that his body was free of all sickness. He would have loved to spend the day with his friends. But at least he had his phone.

He grabbed it from the bedside table and the messages started flying. After a few minutes he had learnt that Michael, Max, Lloyd and Jake were going to miss school in order to be at Poppy's bail hearing.

The day passed slowly. Doctors and nurses came and went. Test results started coming back showing that he was fine. To Elz that sounded like a good reason to let him go. To the doctors that sounded like a good reason for more tests.

He was getting updates from the boys but there was little happening - Poppy didn't seem likely to come before the judge until the afternoon.

His mother came in for a couple of hours, but they mostly succeeded in annoying each other. She could see that he was well, and didn't see any need to hang around and make him and herself miserable. So she left after lunch.

But after 2:30pm his phone started filling up with messages. As Poppy's bail hearing began, Michael was sending him factual updates, while Jake was describing which people looked like which animals. Elz was outraged that Poppy could be in trouble for what she had done. He thought she should get a Nobel Prize or something, not a prison sentence. As the updates kept coming he got more and more worried. If she ended up in jail he would do anything to get her out. She had saved his life - the least he could do was to serve her in her hour of need.

He was worried when he got the message that Poppy sacked the lawyer whose head looked like a porcupine. He was even more worried when he got the message that the prosecutor with giraffe's legs was opposing bail. He was more worried again when the judge with a chimpanzee's mouth was getting more and more upset.

But just when it got to the climax of the case everything changed. In the one instance two things happened.

There was a massive clap of thunder. He had never heard thunder so loud - the whole building shook from it.

His ears rang from the massive sound.

But there was no need to ask where the lightning bolt struck, because in that same moment another sound began. A loud crack was followed by another straight away, and then still more, all on top of one another. They seemed to be coming from above him. Elz then saw something move out of the corner of his eye. He looked at the glass wall and saw a crack in the glass. It went the entire length of the window in his room. The cracking sounds got louder, and within seconds there were thousands of them, coming from every direction.

All of a sudden his window was covered in dozens of cracks, with more appearing every second. Elz realised this was bad.

Without thinking he moved as far from the window as he could get. He stared at it with wide eyes. The change in sound was what filled him with dread the most. From the floors above him the sound of glass smashing and people screaming got louder and louder. He saw a shard of glass near the floor of his room, and then in just a few seconds the whole lot went. Elz screamed as *Purple Angels* shattered into a million pieces.

In an instant the entire wall crumbled, and countless pieces of glass crashed to the ground. An entire side of the building was exposed. Elz screamed and instinctively pushed himself further up his bed and away from the window. The elements raced in - rain was being blown in by the strong wind.

Everything in the room was getting wet. There were pieces of broken glass all over the floor of his room. The cold hit him hard, but he barely noticed it, such was the shock he was in. He could hear screams from all directions. He was on the third floor, so he didn't dare go anywhere near the edge to look out.

With his heart beating almost out of his chest, Elz knew he had to get out of there. From his bed he reached down and was able to get his shoes. He could barely put them on because his hands were trembling so much. He got off his bed, and stuck as close as possible to the back wall, as far from the gaping hole as he could. He made it to the door. He opened it and stepped into the corridor.

As soon as he stepped into it, he wasn't sure which was worse. There was absolute panic everywhere. Patients were collapsed on the floor, looking terrified. Unlike Elz, most of them were very sick, as well as being very frightened.

Some had cuts from the glass. Staff were running around trying to avoid shattered glass. There were some voices shouting and others screaming. No one knew what to do - when had something like this ever happened before?

Elz saw the sign for the stairs and just thought that with a wall missing the best place to be is as low down as possible. He dodged the people running up and down the corridor. As he opened the door to the stairwell, a doctor he had spoken to just an hour ago bumped into him. The doctor said, "Elz, it's not safe here. The whole building will be evacuated. It's best if you just go. You're not sick. You're free to leave." Elz said, "OK." He didn't need to be told twice. Elz raced down the steps, dodging panicked people everywhere.

The ground floor was even more chaotic. The building was half surrounded by purple, red and blue broken glass. The main entrance was on the side of the building that had *Purple Angels* above it, so that entrance was effectively closed. Elz joined a stampede of people heading for a smaller exit on a different side of the building. There were people screaming and the wind and rain were pushing into the main foyer. Staff were running everywhere, and some of them were shouting at the crowd of people to keep moving and to reach the exit. By simply following the main flow of people Elz found himself moving towards a door. The crush of people was immense. Everyone was desperate to get out. Elz joined the crush, kept his legs moving and in a moment he was through.

Having burst out of the hospital he stood in the rain, as more and more people were coming out. Those who were well enough simply tried to find a building nearby to stay dry.

Elz then realised that he still had his phone in his left hand. He looked at it. There was a two word message from Michael, 'Bail denied.' He had forgotten all about Poppy's case during the ten minutes of mayhem in the hospital.

In an instant Elz knew he had to get there. The court was on the same street as the hospital - one of the main roads in that part of London. But it was probably a mile away. So he ran. It was a cold April day, and he was only wearing a tee shirt and jeans. The rest of his clothes were back on the third floor of the hospital. He didn't care. He didn't even notice the cold. He just started running.

The footpaths were crowded. The streets were heavy with traffic because on a London afternoon they always are.

But in addition it seemed that every ambulance in the city was coming towards the hospital. He ran across intersections, he dodged prams, shoppers and tourists. He hadn't run at full speed for almost a year, and it felt wonderful. The rain was teeming. It soaked right through his shirt in no time at all. He ran on, and could see the court building coming closer. The red double decker buses were actually so stuck in traffic that Elz was overtaking them rather than the other way around. He had done his best to sprint the whole mile to the court.

When he finally ran to the steps of the building people were coming out. He slowed down - he was utterly exhausted. There was a lady who seemed to be the centre of people's attention. Elz looked at her and even though he had never met her before, he knew who she was - Poppy certainly looked a lot like her mum. "Mrs Joshua!" Elz called out. He took two huge breaths and tried again, louder, "Mrs Joshua!"

The whole group that she was with stopped. Elz stepped up to speak to her. She was crying, and looked a mess. "I'm Elz." Three deep breaths. "Poppy healed me." Three deep breaths. "I don't have cancer anymore." Three deep breaths, and then the emotion hit Elz as well. "I'm so sorry!" With that he burst into tears. Until now, Elz had not processed the emotions he had gone through.

He was dead, and now he lived. He had cheated death by beating cancer and then again by beating the catastrophe at the hospital. The relief hit him like a flood. He didn't know why it all bubbled up in him as he stood on the pavement in the rain, meeting Poppy's mother. But the tears flowed, even though it was the last thing that he had planned.

As a mother Miriam Joshua instinctively reached out for him. She didn't care that he was soaked. The two of them stood there on the footpath, crying and embracing. They had never met before, but their lives were now bound together.

She spoke to him, "I'm glad you're well Elz." She found a tiny bit of comfort - she was embracing the proof that her daughter had made a difference in his life.

The rain continued to tumble down. Someone put an umbrella over them.

After they had cried and embraced they went their separate ways. Both went back to their own homes. Neither of them knew what to do next.

Chapter Sixteen

Tim Harrop

Saturday dawned, cold and bleak. Michael, Max, Lloyd and Jake each woke up with a mood that matched the weather. They couldn't bear the thought of what Poppy might be going through right now. None of them were interested in video games, sleeping in, or the day's football matches - the kinds of things that normally interested them on a Saturday morning. Each of them reached for his phone, and a volley of messages flew back and forth.

The boys got together around ten in the morning.

Elz was with them. They made their way to the local fast food restaurant and ended up at table on the top floor, right at the back and away from everyone else. There were few people upstairs at that time of day anyway. Most of them sucked on a drink. No one really knew what to say. But they sure knew that they wanted to stay together in a moment like this. None of them could bear the thought of being alone.

The rain still fell, although not as heavily as yesterday. Every time the conversation strayed away from the events of the last two days it soon died. Other things simply didn't matter. Every now and then one of them would comment on something that happened, usually to criticise Mrs Pilot for something she had said. Or the judge. Or the prosecutor. But mostly Mrs Pilot.

Michael was on his phone - most of them were - and he scrolled through his social media news. It was the usual stuff - pictures of parties, cat videos and the usual gossip. The viral video of the moment was a guy throwing things over his shoulder into different containers. That was it. It was either fake or it took hundreds of takes. Or he had someone teeking out of camera shot. Seriously - some clown somewhere makes the most simple and ridiculous video and it was being watched by millions of people around the planet. Now the guy is fending off dozens of requests for interviews and his friends think he is a legend. Michael kept scrolling. There were more videos of young kids doing cute things, people hurting themselves, pets being cute, various teeking tricks, all of it just regular people who happened to organise or film something funny. But then a thought came to him. Maybe they could start something. Maybe they could use social media to make people take notice of what had happened.

"Hey, we could start something today," he said more to himself than to any of the others. Lloyd and Jake were talking to each other, and didn't hear. "Hey, shut up!" Still they kept talking. Michael raised his voice, "Shut up!" Both boys turned their heads. Lloyd answered, "You shut up!" It was the 14-year-old boy equivalent of, "Yes, what is it?"

"No, listen" Michael continued, "Look, how much strife do you think we could make today?"

Max was confused. "You wanna fight someone?"

"No!" Michael replied. "I mean how much strife can we make online, you idiot. Look, what happened to Poppy is wrong. It's rubbish. She should be a hero, not a prisoner. But we can't get her out of jail. We can't do anything physically. But maybe we can make chaos online. We can get people talking.

I mean, Elz, you sure got people talking on Thursday afternoon. I think we owe it to her. I want the whole world to know that an innocent kid is in jail here because some morons were too stupid to realise that the world needs less cancer, not more. If we can't do anything useful, let's at least the hell go down swinging."

"But what you wanna do?" Max replied.

"I want to spend today making Poppy famous. I want to fill the internet with Poppy Joshua. This is Poppy's day, and I want to make a riot on her behalf."

There was a brief silence as the idea hung in the balance.

"We could do that." said Lloyd.

"Well come on then!" said Elz. The others were in agreement too. It might not amount to much, but it was the only thing they could do. The plan was the right one.

Michael continued, "Empty your pockets onto the table." Jake said, "Huh?" "I said empty your damn pockets onto the table! Let's see what we've got." The boys emptied their pockets, although most of them weren't sure why this was needed. Michael surveyed the table.

"Right. Listen to me - we've got one day, five phones, three chargers, four packets of chewing gum, seven meal vouchers, and free wi-fi. Let's go for it!"

Like soldiers coming out of the trenches the boys headed off to war. They were seeking to inflict maximum virtual damage on the world that had put Poppy Joshua in jail. But instead of rifles, these young soldiers were armed with mobile phones. It wasn't about bullets and land, it was all about pixels and eyeballs.

Elz knew that he could start it. His post on Thursday had had a huge response - people from all over the world bothered to comment on it. He started to type, telling what had happened to him, but then he realised what was needed.

He turned to his left, "Jake, video me." Thrusting his phone at Jake he stood up and prepared to speak.

Jake instantly knew it was the right idea. He said, "Elz over here, near the window - light's better." Jake started filming. Elz looked at the phone and started speaking, "So, two days ago I was struggling to survive because of cancer. I was in a wheelchair.

I could barely take more than a few steps on my own. Right now I am totally better. I have perfect health, and it's all because a friend, Poppy Joshua, discovered a way to teek people free of cancer. She should get awards. But instead, she's in jail. So I won't rest until she is set free. She's done nothing wrong - she must go free now!"

Jake uploaded the video. Many of those who saw and responded to his post saw this one as well.

Comments began pouring in. A great many were

cynical, saying that it was all nonsense. But then all of Elz's school friends, in fact everyone who knew him argued back and vouched for what Elz was saying. And with every comment, response or action, the name of Poppy Joshua rose from the floor and began a march up the internet trending names. The battle was joined.

Jake knew that this was what they needed to do all day. Jake decided to do an interview. With the mobile phone camera rolling, he asked Elz for more news. He asked him about the history of his cancer. He asked about the medication that he was on. He asked about what had happened since Thursday afternoon. Elz gave answers with a level of detail that only a genuine cancer patient could provide. Upload.

But Jake knew that he needed entertainment more than information. He put the phone on the ground and hit record. His face appeared on the screen, as he laid on the floor in front of a pair of shoes. "So these shoes belong to my friend Elz. He's about to get down and do some push ups.

How many push ups do you think you can do if you are dying of cancer? Not many. How many can Elz do? Let's find out. Come on then!" The shoes moved back and Elz then came into view. He started doing push ups, and kept going until his arms couldn't take any more and his face was red from the effort.

Jake was right next to him, and did his best army sergeant impersonation. "C'mon cancer boy, are you even trying? All the way down! Keep the back straight!" Upload.

Jake spoke to the camera - "How hard is it to beat a cancer patient in an arm wrestle? Not hard. Come on then." The camera moved to show Elz and Max in an arm wrestle, evenly matched, and both with their faces bursting from the strain. Then back to Jake - "Hmmm, maybe he doesn't have cancer anymore?" Upload.

Jake spoke to the camera again, this time in a whisper, "Is it OK to hurt people who have cancer? Can they fight back? Not really. But watch this."

The camera showed Max creeping up behind Elz and then forcefully flicking his ear with his finger. Elz spun and said, "Hey you jerk!" Max mocked him, "Aww, watcha gonna do about it cancer boy?" The two of them started pushing each other and wrestling, with Elz trying to exact some revenge on Max. They both ended up on the ground, and were wrestling violently with each other. The camera then came back to Jake. "Hmmm, maybe he doesn't have cancer anymore?" Upload.

Jake spoke to the camera, "Question - how fast can a cancer patient get me another napkin?" The camera then turns to Elz, sitting across from Jake. Jake's voice came, "On your marks, get set, go!"

Elz then burst out of his seat and sprinted across the top floor of the restaurant. The camera bounced around and followed him, filming as he flew down the steps, grabbed a napkin from the front counter, and sprinted back up the stairs, taking them two or three at a time. He crashed into his seat with napkin in hand. The camera came back to Jake, "17.3

seconds. Hmmm - maybe he doesn't have cancer anymore?" Upload.

As the videos came online throughout the day, Jake and Elz responded to the comments, fought back against those saying it was fake, and generally did their best to fan the flames. And there were plenty of flames. The videos began to build a huge audience. More and more people were sharing them. Each hour that passed saw thousands take an interest. And then tens of thousands. The boys used the hashtag #freepoppyjoshua to connect their posts. Others began doing the same. Poppy's march up the list of trending names online continued.

When Max first grabbed his phone and headed into battle, he wasn't sure where to start. He was committed to helping Poppy but he was well aware that it was Saturday.

That meant that to do this he would be giving up both playing and watching today's football matches. It wasn't easy for him. But then he realised - football is massively popular, and if he couldn't spend the day watching it, he could at least raise Poppy's profile within it.

One of the boys that played with Max at his club had a father who was a former professional. He started messaging his friend, and linking to the videos as Jake uploaded them.

His friend put out a message in support of Poppy.

Then Max posted to his friend's fathers social media account. Sure enough, an hour or two later, he shared a post about Poppy. With this in place Max could really get started.

Every player who had ever played with his friend's father soon got a message from Max, asking them to share a post about Poppy. But crucially some of these people were still current players. Max bombarded their social media accounts with posts about Poppy. Most ignored them, but a small number responded. After all, they could see that someone they respected was already speaking in support.

The average professional footballer has a social media following that politicians can only dream about. With every single footballer who expressed any support, Poppy's profile leapt. As the day wore on Max was pleased with his progress.

The people he had got to respond had huge followings. The news about Poppy's situation was really spreading.

As the day's matches started, Max followed the scores. The early kick off that day was Manchester United playing against some team from the bottom of the ladder who were just hoping not to get beaten too badly. United did what everyone expected them to, and won a comfortable 2-0 victory. Their centre forward Tim Harrop scored both goals.

And once the match was over, he did what most 21st century footballers do straight after a match - had a shower and checked his social media accounts.

Max didn't know it, but Harrop had lost his brother to cancer when they were both children. On the field he was the boss - the best player for one of the strongest teams. But away from the cameras and the publicity, he thought of his brother often. It was 11 years ago. It was the only thing that had really gone wrong in his otherwise perfect life. But it left a scar in his heart that was deeper than anyone knew.

So when he flicked through the hundreds of posts people had put on his page, the word 'cancer' grabbed his attention. He stopped scrolling and read Max's message. It resonated with him. He had no idea if healing someone from cancer was possible or not. But he personally knew, at the bottom of his heart, that curing cancer would be the greatest thing that could happen on Earth. Suddenly scoring two goals in today's match didn't seem as important.

He tapped out, "This girl should not be in jail! #freepoppyjoshua". He put his phone down. As his teammates walked past, some of them wondered why he wasn't grinning as he normally would be after a win.

A few minutes later, Max saw the message. His eyes went as wide as dinner plates. His hand started to tremble.

Never in all his life did he expect to have a personal interaction with Tim Harrop. He jumped out of his seat, "Guys, guys, guys! No way! LISTEN! So I sent a message to every footballer playing in the early match today. So Tim Harrop, yes, THE Tim Harrop, has just written this -" and he read the quote. The whole group was stunned. Then they erupted, just like the fans in the stadium had earlier for Harrop's goals.

Michael, Lloyd and Elz all instinctively leaped out of their seats and reached for Max's phone to see if it was for real. They wouldn't believe it until they saw it with their own eyes. It was real alright. Jake, however, just sat there saying, "Who's Tim Harrop?" The others ignored him for the moment. They were too excited to stop and fill him in. Max stood with his arms in the air, hooting and hollering, and drawing looks from the other people in the restaurant. But Max didn't care about that - Max was mates with Tim Harrop. Five hours ago they had set out to create electronic mayhem, and now they had the Manchester United centre forward chiming in with a message of support. Harrop's social media following was as big as the entire population of London. And it was worldwide. In a single moment, their reach had gone from tens of thousands to tens of millions.

They were winning. They kept up the attack.

When Lloyd first started, he thought that what people really wanted is proof. Just because someone makes a claim about being better, well, how is anyone meant to know if it is true or not? So he called out to Elz, "Hey, what was that doctor who told you to leave the hospital?"

"Andrews, Doctor Andrews."

Lloyd found him on the hospital website. Ten minutes later he found the doctor's social media page. Lloyd posted on it, "Hey doc, you know that the girl who healed your cancer patient is in jail for doing it? Do you go to prison when someone gets better? #freepoppyjoshua."

For the first hour, Lloyd mainly posted on his own page, and tried to increase interest in other posts the boys had made. But around the middle of the day he got a private message from the doctor.

Doctor Andrews didn't spend much time on social media but he did see Lloyd's message straight away. Normally he would spend a Saturday morning out cycling or running.

But today he stayed close to his phone and his email. He wasn't meant to be working but the evacuation meant that everything was crazy. All his patients had been relocated to different hospitals, and he wanted to keep track of who was going where. He was intrigued by what had happened to Elz. Doctor Andrews loved teeking. He marvelled at it. It was the most unexpected scientific breakthrough of his lifetime, and the scientist in him was amazed that so much of it was still unexplained. He was also intrigued by the obvious question that no one spent much time discussing - if teeking is possible then what else can human beings do that we don't know about yet?

Doctor Andrews did his best with Elz. He was a young doctor but he knew enough to know that Elz would die. He had seen many cancer patients in their final months.

He was familiar with how the progress of the tumours worked. There were 'remissions' - stages when the progress seemed to pause. The patient would maintain their condition for a season.

But then the sickness would worsen again. What Doctor Andrews saw in Elz was radically different. The boy looked cancer free, acted cancer free and the scans were cancer free. He was cancer free. Doctor Andrews had never seen anything like it before. After hearing the story about what his schoolmate had done, Doctor Andrews was amazed.

It left the tantalising possibility that he himself was in the middle of an astonishing medical breakthrough. Even though he was trying to keep track of his moving patients, his thoughts kept coming back to Elz.

So when the message from Lloyd arrived, Doctor Andrews dropped everything. He was stunned that a 14-year-old girl was in jail right now. This girl might have made history, and she was in a cell! Half a dozen phone calls later he replied to Lloyd's message:

"Hello Lloyd. I have spent this morning looking into the issue you raised. I was treating your friend, Eleazar, and I can confirm that after running tests subsequent to his admission on Thursday his body is cancer free. I have no explanation for how this happened. I am informed that some kind of teeking might have been involved. I am very concerned that someone is in prison because of this incident.

As far as I can tell this might be a significant medical breakthrough. It is certainly not, in my opinion, anything that should be punished. I shall raise this issue with my superiors at the hospital."

The doctor wasn't stopping there. Next, he called his boss and explained the situation. Then his boss's boss. Even though it was a Saturday, they were all available because they were all on the phone trying to sort out the consequences of the evacuation. Doctor Andrews found that he was getting good responses. No one liked hearing that a 14-year-old girl was in jail. It was easy to raise sympathy for her. Every manager and executive he spoke to realised what might flow if Doctor Andrews was right. If this boy's surprising turnaround was some sort of cancer breakthrough, then it would put the hospital on the map. Their hospital would be famous - well, famous for something other than having lightning destroy a beautiful wall. And if they were wrong, well at least a young girl might get out of jail. There was no down-side.

After a couple of hours of phone calls, checking, double checking, and getting permission from Elz's family, the hospital chief executive released a statement. It said that Elz was cancer free, and that the hospital was "deeply concerned that someone had been imprisoned for causing this remarkable improvement in the patient's health." Doctor Andrews couldn't believe that he had got the hospital management to fall in line so quickly. He messaged Lloyd with a link to the statement.

Lloyd instantly realised he had hit gold. He methodically went through every single cynical response to any post and linked to the hospital's short statement. When the treating hospital says that the patient is cancer free, who can argue? Who knows better? Lloyd made sure that the internet was covered in links to the statement.

When Michael first grabbed his phone, he wondered where to start. Some school lesson had taught him that when you want to complain about something, your member of parliament can help.

So he did a search to find out who his member of parliament, or MP, was. A few minutes later he posted onto their social media page, "Hey rodsmithmp - since when did you guys pass a law against healing people with cancer? #freepoppyjoshua"

Realising that was quite easy, Michael thought that perhaps he should post to the other members of parliament.

He asked the internet how many there were. His heart sunk when the answer came back - 650! But then he thought of Poppy in jail. And so, throughout the morning,

650 MPs each got a message, and 650 staff members who check social media for the MPs they work for, became aware of Poppy's case. There were even a few MPs who commented themselves in reply. Some had heard about Elz and Poppy during the day, and made pretty simple promises to look into it.

Once the hospital put out their statement, Michael went back to his MP and all 649 others as well. "Hey rodsmithmp - if the hospital says our friend is better, why is the one who made him better behind bars?" Then he gave them the link to the statement on the hospital website at the bottom of his message. Throughout the afternoon 650 staff members who monitor the social media accounts of their MP's noted that this was worth looking into if the hospital was making statements about it.

And of course one of those 650 MPs is the Prime Minister himself. His staff noticed the message, and the rising level of discussion around the country about Poppy Joshua.

During the afternoon the shift manager for a major social media company noted the growing number of references to Poppy Joshua. He was always curious when something new emerged. The afternoon's talk was being dominated by celebrity romances, a new Hollywood blockbuster, football and the Royal Family, but Poppy Joshua didn't seem connected to any of that. He marvelled as it trended higher and higher as the afternoon wore on.

By the end of his shift it seemed the whole country was talking about Poppy Joshua, and a good bit of the rest of the world as well.

Around 6pm the boys left the restaurant. They had put in a long day. They set out to create digital mayhem and they had been outstandingly successful. Poppy was famous.

She had pushed all manner of celebrities off the top of the social media charts.

The professional publicists that are paid to get their clients noticed, had been schooled by some teenage boys, who had nothing but five phones, three chargers, four packets of chewing gum, seven meal vouchers, and free wi-fi.

As they walked home, the fire that they had started continued to blaze. Discussion continued, videos were made, memes and animations were created. Even traditional media started to look into it, just as they had with Danielle Tunupingu all those years ago.

And as Poppy lay in her cell, she had no idea that any of it had happened.

Chapter Seventeen

The Three Ministers

On Sunday morning the Prime Minister King flicked through the newspapers, spending three minutes on each. The fact that the Prime Minister had the surname "King" was a source of endless amusement to the British press and the British people. The internet was always full of jokes and memes playing on the fact. His family thought it was even funnier. At every family wedding, funeral or special occasion the "King of Kings" jokes came thick and fast.

Prime Minister King was not that old but he seemed to have been Prime Minister for a long time. He had gone into politics when he was very young, and seemed to have a brilliant ability to be in the right place at the right time.

When other politicians were full of ambition and cunning, he had the skills, smarts and plain good luck to watch them knock each other out and then be the last one standing. When events looked as though they were working against him, something would change, and with perfect timing the sun would be shining on his decisions just in time for the next election.

One of his nicknames was 'the smiling Prime Minister' because he went through life with such a bounce in his step and a broad grin on his face. It wasn't an act - he truly loved what he did. He loved Sunday mornings in particular - less people around, less rules about what you had to do, and more time to reflect on all the decisions to be made.

When you are a President, Prime Minister, or somehow or other in charge of a country, you don't get days off. There are only busy days and extremely busy days. The Prime Minister was happy that he would have a busy day today, in contrast with the super-busy nature of his average weekday.

As he flicked through the papers, he noted that every single one of them ran a story about Poppy Joshua, whom he had never heard of. Most of them picked up on the link to the London Children's Cancer Hospital, the damage to which had dominated Saturday's news.

He called his Chief of Staff, James Cardle, which was normal for a Sunday morning. A Prime Minister's Chief of Staff doesn't really have days off either.

"Good morning, Prime Minister."

"James my man - what's new in the world?" The "my man" was the Prime Minister's acknowledgement that talking on a Sunday should be less formal than the rest of the week.

"So the French election result is in line with expectations, and I've arranged you to call…" and on he went, mentioning various issues.

The Prime Minister listened for a few moments, and then became bored. He interrupted - "So what do you know about this Poppy Joshua situation?"

"Yes, Prime Minister, I note a number of press articles discussing it. It was prominent on social media yesterday. A number of MPs have messaged me to ask if we have anything to say. It's fast moving - all happened in the last few days. Might be worth waiting for a bit to see if it blows over. The last thing we want to do is to be seen to be soft on inside teeking."

"Hmmm, yes. But no one seems to have been hurt, have they?"

"Not at this stage Prime Minister, but you just don't know if the boy might take a turn for the worse later on, or something like that."

"Hmmm, the hospital put out a statement though, didn't they? I think I will have a talk to Liz and Stephen about it. Find out what they are doing and make it happen later today."

"Yes, Prime Minister."

One hour and a short talk to the new French President later, James told the Prime Minister that Liz Davidson, the Minister for Justice, and Stephen Sparks, the Minister for Teeking, were both in London that afternoon, and would come in at 2pm.

-

"Afternoon Liz, afternoon Stephen. How're things?"

The Prime Minister didn't wait for a reply. "So Liz, what do you know about the Poppy Joshua matter?"

"Well Prime Minister I have a transcript of the bail application from Friday, which I've read. It seems that on a technical understanding of the law, it is right that bail was denied. She failed to give the assurances that she wouldn't do it again. She showed some strength - my goodness she's got some backbone. But it is a very harsh outcome on a 14-year-old girl. She'll likely have to wait at least a year for a trial. But the charges should probably be dropped if no harm has been suffered. At the time of the bail hearing the young man, Eleazar, was in hospital, just being monitored. But he has since been discharged. There is no evidence that he was hurt. To the contrary, well, ..."

She didn't really know how to describe what had happened to Elz. She wasn't used to telling the Prime Minister about miraculous healings. They usually talked about budgets. Her sentence therefore died when it was just barely started, which was a bit awkward.

The Prime Minister jumped into the paused conversation, sidestepping the dead sentence. "So, the hospital have released a statement saying that he's better. That's a bit unusual. But it does mean we can have confidence that he's better."

"Yes, Prime Minister. Now section 77 of the Teeking Act does give you the power to have teeking charges dropped.

Obviously, it is not possible for you to be looking over the prosecutor's shoulders on every decision that they make, but in rare circumstances you might want to intervene.

There is not much doubt that these are rare circumstances. Of course, in matters such as this, we have never before gone over the prosecutors' heads. I don't think the power has ever been used. It might not be well received, so - "

"You know Liz, I'm more worried about the young girl in prison than the prosecutors who are at home on the couch reading a book or watching TV."

"Yes. I think we all should be."

The Prime Minister turned to face his teeking minister. "Stephen, how do you understand it?"

"Prime Minister, the essence of teeking is moving things. Inside teeking is feared because people are worried that moving things inside the body will result in harm being done. I guess there are situations where you could move something inside the body to make it better - to reset a broken bone perhaps. But the reports of this situation are nothing like that. This is a situation where cancer was, erm, well, it was healed, it seems. It is not clear if anything moved.

In fact it seems that it didn't. There is nothing that, if moved, could produce the outcome that the boy experienced.

When I add all this together, I think we are dealing with something beyond teeking. This is a new development.

It's based on the power that the macadamia nuts contain, but it is a new thing entirely. There have been other reports of people doing strange things after eating the nuts.

Some of them are from the aboriginal tribe in Australia where this all started. I wouldn't even call what we are dealing with here teeking. How can it be? Nothing moved."

The three of them paused and let the idea sink in.

Prime Minister King said, "Not teeking? If that's the case then this is a significant development. This could be a whole new discovery, and a critical one at that."

Another pause. Their minds raced.

"Wow" said Stephen, softly. "If that's the case, then this girl could be Britain's answer to Danielle Tunupingu. I really think that the last place she should be is in prison."

The Prime Minister seized on the idea. "Yes! In fact, we have to make a decision. Do we want to be the government that goes down in history as the ones who put Poppy Joshua behind bars? When we discovered the person who has the cure for cancer, we were the fools who put her in jail? If we do that, they will still be talking about us in 200 years time, but not in the way that we all hope!"

Liz spoke up, "Prime Minister, as I said earlier, under the teeking laws you have the power to drop the charges and release her from jail. Using that power will upset some people, no doubt about that. But the power is yours, if you want to act."

"And should I?"

Liz carefully thought about her answer. She slowly said, "I recommend that you have the charges dropped and Miss Joshua be released today."

"Hmmm. Stephen?"

"I agree with that recommendation, Prime Minister. I can't see what she has done wrong. To have her reunited with her family today is surely the right thing to do here."

The Prime Minister never needed long to make up his mind. "The three of us are in agreement then. I'll instruct that the papers be drawn up immediately. Miss Joshua can spend the night in her own home. Where this all leads, I have no idea. I think we could be on the edge of history being made."

The meeting was finished, and they each left. James Cardle had been in the meeting, taking notes. As he and the Prime Minister walked through the corridors he said, "Prime Minister, I'm worried that you have not taken into the account the sensitivities of the police in this matter. To use such a power could create a powerful opponent."

"James, I don't really care about their sensitivities.

They will have to cope. Releasing the girl is the right thing to do. The three of us were in complete agreement. We are acting as one. That's the end of it. Have the papers organised immediately."

"Yes, Prime Minister."

As their paths diverged, Prime Minister King had another thought. "James" he called out. "Put out a press release as well."

"Yes, Prime Minister."

Half an hour later Prime Minister King signed the first ever Section 77 order, ordering the release of Poppy Joshua from prison.

Chapter Eighteen

Phil

In the cells under the Charlton courthouse it was calm. The guard on duty enjoyed the Sunday afternoon shift. There wasn't much hassle, there wasn't much action, and he got paid higher rates for working weekends. He was surprised when the phone started ringing. He teeked the receiver into his hand, and a familiar voice spoke to him.

"Hey Phil, its Chelsea from head office. Now I'm sure you're flat out busy with the usual Sunday afternoon madness. Is that teek sports on the radio I can hear? ... I'm sure you are going flat out down there mate, I'm sure you are ... So you've got a Poppy Joshua there at the moment. The kid who's been all over the internet, right ... Yeah, yeah that's the one. So I just got a message from the department that she has been granted an immediate release under Section 77... no, Section 77 ... yeah, I had to look it up too. But I've got the order here, and it's personally signed by the Prime Minister. I'm not kidding. Friends in high places this kid has, but I'm emailing it through to you right now ... No, I've never seen one before either. I think I've never seen one because there's never been one. So there you go my friend I've just emailed through a bit of history for you. You got that now? ... Yeah so the procedure is an immediate release. It's not to wait till tomorrow. You've got to process it straight away … It's visitors from 4 to 5, yeah? Should be able to get it done before then … No, nothing else is needed. It's been signed off by everyone else. You can call her up straight away, roll the door, let her out, do what you do. At least the rain's stopped … Oh I know they took away some of the romance when they put the door on hinges rather than wheels, but what can you do? Roll the door, open the door, whatever, just make sure she's on the other side of it to where she is now. I will leave it in your capable hands. You're a good man, Phil."

Phil got off the phone and printed off the order. He scratched his head - it was the first such order he had seen.

He got his keys and ambled down the corridor to Poppy's cell. "So, Poppy Joshua?" Poppy didn't have time to reply. But he knew who she was. "I've got some good news for you, kid. See this?" Phil held up his copy of the order. "They just sent it through to me. It says that all charges are withdrawn, and you are free to go home. Bet you weren't expecting that. But that's what it says. So come on then, let's get you on your way." He started fumbling with his keys.

Poppy said nothing. The shock was too great. She had been lying on her bed, the same top bunk that she had first slept on, even though she now had the whole cell to herself.

She sat up when Phil starting talking but she didn't say anything.

Her mouth was open, it's just that no words were coming out. Poppy's mind couldn't compute the words she was hearing. She had emotionally readied herself for a year or so in jail. And yet here it was, the third day that she had seen the inside of the prison, and she was free? It couldn't possibly be true.

Phil was now standing at the door, which was open. Then the thought hit her - get out! Get out right now! She flew off the bed, scurried down the ladder and burst out into the corridor. She stood there looking back at where she had just been.

The cell had swallowed her on Friday but she had beaten it on Sunday. Her tongue was working again and the words started to pour out. "Really? How come? What's happened? I can't believe it. Oh, I want to go home. You are serious, right? I want to be home so much. I'm going home!"

Phil got a kick out of her excitement. It was nice to have something good to tell someone - which was not what being a prison guard generally gave you. He let Poppy babble on as they walked down the corridor together. Poppy's heel was now better, and gave her no problem walking. He assured her that it was for real, and no, he didn't know why it had happened. Poppy's excitement only increased as they went along. He went through all the normal procedures. She got back into her regular clothes. He gave her the bag that she had brought in with her, and the standard ten pounds in cash to get home.

When everything was in order, he smiled at her and said, "All ready?" He opened the final door. Poppy looked through and could see the pavement outside the building.

"So, I'm free to go?" Phil assured her, "Yes you are -

out you go, and good luck to you. You've got no idea how famous you are."

And with that, Poppy stepped through the door. She was free.

Poppy could not believe how beautiful the wind felt on her face. She began to cry, but these were tears of happiness. The rain had stopped but the streets were still wet.

It was fairly cold but Poppy didn't care. Being a Sunday afternoon the city didn't have the hustle that it often did. But that just made it all the more beautiful. Poppy had never dreamt that standing on a pavement could be such a glorious experience. What Phil had said about being famous made no sense, so she put it out of her mind.

Her phone was out of charge. She would have loved to call her mum. But she decided to just get home and give the rest of the family the surprise of their lives. The courthouse was on a main road. All she had to do to get home was to catch a bus for a couple of miles, and then it was a short walk. She walked to the bus stop and waited. The smile wouldn't leave her face. She was free. She realised what a remarkable thing freedom was. She could go in any direction, wherever she wanted, and no one would tell her she couldn't.

There was no street she was forbidden to walk down, no route she was blocked from taking, and no bars or walls to prevent her. A few minutes later she sat on the bus, and it felt like the most beautiful bus trip anyone had ever taken. Everything about the bus was wonderful.

It wasn't crowded, so she had a seat. All these people, all enjoying their freedom to get on and off wherever they wanted. And she was now one of them, just as she had been her whole life apart from those few horrible days.

A couple of the other passengers seemed to be looking at her. She wondered if there was something about her appearance ... she knew that she didn't look glamorous, but that's what two nights in jail will do to you.

Her heart started to beat faster and the bus approached her stop. A smile broke out on her face to see the familiar streets and homes. As she walked down her street, her speed picked up. Within seconds she had broken out into a run. She flew past the houses of her neighbours. She was getting close, and her emotions were now running as fast as her legs. The tears had already started to come. Her house was now in view, but she couldn't see her mum's car. She hoped desperately that someone was home. She ran up to the door and her heart sang - it opened.

Her reunion with her brother James and sister Olivia was beautiful. They hugged as they had never hugged before.

Olivia cried, and James was trying hard not to. But she ached to see her mum.

Miriam Joshua was trying to cope with what was happening to her daughter. But she wasn't coping. How could anyone cope under such circumstances? On Sunday afternoon she left the other two kids at home and set off to visit Poppy in prison. She had been constantly fighting back tears ever since Thursday night, but since Friday afternoon in particular. If she could at least see Poppy this afternoon, she might keep it together for a little bit. Maybe.

Miriam drove her little Ford through London's streets. At least there was not so much traffic on a Sunday. The Charlton Courthouse was all closed up save for one little side door on weekends. She made her way through the door to where some other visitors were gathered in a small, ugly room.

Not that any of the visitors were aware of the ugliness - they were all just desperate to see their loved ones.

Phil was at the counter. In a few minutes Miriam was at the front of the short queue. Phil spoke to her. "Who are you here to see, love?"

"Poppy Joshua - my daughter." Her heart was racing knowing that Poppy was just a few metres away.

"Oh right. Well, I've a question for you then - why do you seek the free amongst the prisoners? She's been released, all charges dropped, you see."

"What?"

"Yes, I'm serious. Just 20 minutes ago I'd say it was. So this order came through from head office, she's been released as all charges have been withdrawn, under Section 77, which means it's direct from the Prime Minister himself. Very unusual. I've got a copy here... there you go you can keep that. But like I said, she walked out of here 20 minutes ago. That's her prison clothes all folded up there on the shelf. She's free. So I can't help you right now!" He smiled.

Miriam was too stunned to smile back. "Well, where has she gone?"

"Oh she was super keen to get back home. She was saying that she was really looking forward ..."

Phil didn't bother finishing that sentence because as soon as he had said the word "home" Miriam Joshua had spun on her heels and headed for the door. She clutched the print out of the Section 77 order. Flying past the others in the queue she started to run. She jumped into the car and started it up. Normally she was a cautious driver, but this was not a normal day. She screeched the tyres as she headed off, and drove like a racing car driver. She had never thrown a car so violently around London's streets. Possibly no one had.

Turning into her own street her heart beat raced faster still. She hurriedly parked the car. As soon as she was out of it she yelled, "Poppy!" She ran to her door, "Poppy!" The door flew open, "Poppy!" "Mum!" came the reply. Poppy flew into her mother's arms. They cried, embraced, cried some more and wouldn't let go. For what seemed like an age they stood and delighted in each other's presence.

"I'm free mum, I'm really free." The other two kids joined in and the four of them stood like a weeping pillar in the doorway of the house. They were the happiest family in all of London.

For the rest of the day the four of them stayed in their living room. They couldn't bear the thought of not being all together, so no one retreated upstairs or even into the kitchen.

Eventually Poppy got online and told all her friends what had happened. No one could believe it. She even included a photo of the Section 77 order.

Then the messages really started flying when news reports appeared about her. Poppy was astounded to see the campaign that Michael, Max, Lloyd, Jake and Elz had launched. The more time she spent on her phone the more she was stunned at how far her fame had grown, all thanks to what they had done.

There were literally millions of people across the world following the story. Her release from prison kept the story going, and the interest seemed to only increase. Some of Poppy's friends started giving out her number to people, and calls and messages began to flood in. The internet simply couldn't get enough of Poppy Joshua.

But Poppy Joshua had had enough of the internet. She just wanted to be with her family. She put her phone down and cuddled up to her mother.

As her head hit the pillow at the end of the day Poppy was exhausted. She had never dreamed that such an emotional roller coaster could exist. And on top of everything that had happened, she had a school day tomorrow. She had no idea how she could possibly concentrate on a school lesson. But that would be tomorrow's problem. For now she rejoiced in being in her home, in her bedroom, on her bed, with her head on her pillow. The sights, smells and feel of her bed and her bedroom were like a palace. There was no place in the world that she would have traded that bedroom for. Her heart overflowed with joy. It was a magnificent feeling to end a magnificent day.

Chapter Nineteen

Lloyd's Father

Michael, Max, Lloyd and Jake were elated. The response to their campaign had been beyond their wildest dreams. They messaged each other on Sunday night, and the tone was one of triumph and victory.

They were so delighted that they decided to meet at Poppy's house on Monday morning, and walk to school together.

They wanted to arrive together, preferably with Mrs Pilot watching, and see the reaction from the rest of the students. They felt like conquering soldiers returning after a famous victory, and they wanted it to look that way as much as possible.

The next morning Poppy woke up feeling brilliant.

She had slept well, and she bounced out of bed. Her usual school morning routine felt like a pleasure, and the rest of her family were the most wonderful people she had ever seen. "You don't know what you've got till it's gone" she thought to herself.

The first that she knew that anything was going on was when her brother James called out, "Who are the people outside?" Her mother wandered over to the window. "Poppy it's your friends! The boys who helped you! And some other people."

Poppy quickly finished getting ready, and rushed outside. She smiled and hugged the four boys. Tears hit the back of Poppy's eyes as she looked at the four of them. She hugged each in turn and said, "Thank you so much. Thank you for everything you have done." The boys were desperate for more information - they threw questions at her about prison, about how she got out, about everything that happened since they saw her dragged away at the end of the bail hearing.

Poppy answered as best she could but there were so many questions all coming on top of one another. And she had plenty of her own as well - she had seen some of what they had done on Saturday but she wanted to know more.

Miriam also emerged from the door and smiled broadly. The day was sunny and mild. The rain was finished.

Miriam also hugged and thanked each of them. She would do anything for those boys - she owed her daughter's freedom to them. After they had both taken it all in, Miriam noticed that they were not moving and not looking like they were about to. She said to the group, "Off you all go. Talk and walk. Have a good day." After they were all about 10 paces from her front door, Poppy raced back. She embraced her mum with a great hug and said, "Love you mum." Then she ran back to the boys. Miriam tried not to cry, but she failed.

As they headed off towards the school, Lloyd introduced the other couple of people who were there. He said to Poppy, "So Poppy this is my dad, he's a teek scientist. He wants to ask you a million dumb questions and be majorly embarrassing to me. I couldn't talk him into doing it some other time. Sorry." Poppy laughed. She didn't think it was embarrassing for Lloyd at all. But she sure wouldn't have wanted her mother doing the same thing.

Lloyd's dad ignored the insult and spoke to Poppy, "Poppy I'm very pleased to meet you. This is my colleague at the university, Doctor Cleopas.

The two of us are most intrigued by what has happened to you over the last few days. Would you be happy to tell us a bit about how these events have unfolded?"

"Sure!" Poppy replied. Even though she had never met them before, she felt comfortable with them, and with the four boys there as well.

As they walked to school, Poppy went through all the events of the previous week. She found herself giving lots of detail about her conversations with Joanna, and about the decisions that she made in the prison. The four boys were content to talk among themselves, and wandered off ahead of Poppy and the two adults.

As Poppy spoke of her remarkable week, she noticed that she had never had people hang on her every word like these two scientists were. They couldn't get enough. It seemed to Poppy that every answer she gave was followed by three more questions. It was fun to explain it all, and to see more people understand what had happened to her - she was only just understanding it herself.

For twenty minutes they walked in the direction of the school, and Poppy explained everything that happened to the two scientists.

As they drew close to the school gate Poppy said goodbye, and re-joined the four boys.

Lloyd's father thanked Poppy profusely for her time.

He even forgot to say goodbye to Lloyd, not that Lloyd was wanting more attention from his father with his school friends around. The scientists were reeling. After Poppy and the boys headed towards the gate, the two of them stopped on the pavement and tried to put it all together.

"That was astonishing. I mean, just remarkable. For ten years all the research in the world has yielded so little..."

"I know!" Dr Cleopas replied. "I feel like I have learnt more in the last 20 minutes than in all my years of study put together. This is what we've been looking for - this is it. I mean, our hearts were burning within us as she explained the character issues! None of us have been looking in that direction, and that seems to be where the answers are."

"True!" Lloyd's father replied, although in reality they were talking over the top of one another, "And for years people have commented on how many teek Olympians are such warm and nice people. Ha! But I mean, nuts that respond to human character - I mean that's so unlikely..."

"But look at the results! Look at what has just happened. No one predicted what happened ten years ago with Danielle, and no one was predicting this. But look at the results. The boy is well. You can't argue with that."

"Some won't want to hear this message, you know. It carries a moral edge. They hate that in our industry."

"Yes, I suppose. Well sod them. Most sick people just want to be well. This is going to be big. This is going to be bigger than big. We've got to study this and see where it leads."

The two scientists continued their talking as the school day began. They were so engrossed in their conversation that they paid no attention to the commotion around the school gate.

As the boys got closer to the gate, they realised that this would be no ordinary morning.

There were all sorts of news crews filming from just outside the grounds, and many of the children did everything they could to be stupid in the background as the cameras were rolling.

But mostly the reporters had formed a large scrum around Elz. He was his normal high-energy self, describing in detail what happened last week, and the cameras were lapping it up.

As soon as people saw the five of them, a crowd formed. Reporters pushed through and put microphones in their faces. But of course Mrs Pilot was nowhere to be seen.

The five of them walked into the school grounds and every student, and in fact every teacher as well, was amazed that someone from their school was now famous. There was such a carnival atmosphere, and nice weather to go along with it, that a few ice cream vans would not have been out of place.

Lots of students had their phones out and were filming it all. Poppy had walked through the grounds of her school most days for the last three years, but now her doing it was something that needed to be captured on video. It made no sense at all. Poppy didn't particularly enjoy all this attention, but she didn't hate it either. It was strange, but she knew one thing for sure - it was a million times better than being in jail.

After a few crazy minutes Poppy was just desperate for something normal to happen, even if it was a boring lesson. But it just so happened that her first subject on a Monday was history, the same as the last lesson she had attended on Thursday. She stopped and marvelled for a minute that it had only been four days since this all started. She felt at least a year older.

As the history lesson began, the whole class was buzzing. All the new celebrities were in the room. Mrs Anderson came in. "Well class, good morning. It's been quite a weekend for some of you. Elz how are you feeling?" "I feel fantastic, Mrs Anderson." He looked it too - the turnaround was astounding.

Mrs Anderson marvelled at him. How could it be the same student that was fighting for his life all these months? It was difficult for her to focus on the lesson at all. "Good. So last week the study of history improved your health significantly, I understand." Everyone laughed. "Might have been that, Miss, might have been" Elz replied.

"So class if we continue with the group work task can the group doing the Black Death promise me that nothing dramatic will happen this time around?" But before any of them could answer someone from the back of the room yelled out, "They'll bring them all back to life!"

"Yes, they just might."

Chapter Twenty

Francois

As Poppy sat in her history class, she was unaware of what she had started. In every country of the world people with cancer are fighting for their lives. And their loved ones desperately want them to survive.

News reports of what happened to her and Elz spread around the world. It was inevitable that some would try to replicate what Poppy had done.

When your family member, friend, loved one, is dying, why not try it? So, many people tried. And some succeeded.

At that exact moment, in a hospital near the city of Mafeking, in South Africa, Francois van Zyl made his way to his wife's bedside. It was a single room. He closed the door and closed the blinds as well. Francois hated the hospital. He hated the noise, the sterility, the smell, the staff who were trying to treat each day like an ordinary working day, when for him there was nothing ordinary going on at all. But mostly he hated the fact that hospitals were needed.

In two weeks time he and Klara would celebrate their golden wedding anniversary - 50 years married. But she wouldn't make it. The cancer was winning. Her body was fighting, but it didn't have much fight left. For almost 50 years it had been his pleasure to be her husband. They had known good times and tough times. They had raised their children, worked hard, and had given far, far more than they ever received. Francois hated lying. In church as a young man he heard a message about keeping your oath even when it hurts, and he had taken it to heart. He had built his character on words like that. Francois meant what he said when he had given his wedding vows, and he had been faithful to them. It had never occurred to him not to be. Klara was the love of his life and he was not ready to be parted from her yet.

He looked at her. She was asleep. She wasn't permanently unconscious yet, but she would be soon.
That morning he had eaten ten macadamia nuts. Then he had a further ten to be sure, and another ten to be doubly sure.

He took his wife's hand. He had read about Poppy Joshua, the schoolgirl in England who had teeked her classmate free from cancer. He cradled Klara's hand in both of his. His tears began to fall. He looked around at the sterile room, with all the medical equipment screaming that everything was not the way it should be.

He had come with the intention of trying to heal her.

He started saying her name over and over, "Klara, Klara, Klara." But in the moment he forgot about that and was overwhelmed with love for her. He sat there in the dark, cradling her hand and telling her that he loved her.

Five minutes later power came from him. Two nurses down the corridor were in the middle of discussion about their shifts for the weekend. "What was that?" the first nurse said. The second didn't answer but they both intuitively started moving down the corridor. Then they heard shouting.

They ran. They burst into Mrs Van Zyl's room and couldn't believe their eyes. A teary Mr Van Zyl was on his feet shouting, "She's better!" And when their eyes turned to the woman in the bed they saw a body that was still frail and elderly, but the eyes - the eyes gave the game away. They were filled with fire, filled with warmth and filled with life the nurses had never seen before.

And before long the internet found out, as it so often does. Within 15 minutes all sorts of doctors and medical staff poured in and out of Klara van Zyl's room. Straight away, one of the social media accounts of a hospital staff member was updated with the words, "I swear what happened to the kids in England with the cancer healing just happened to an old lady in the hospital here. Wow!!!"

Through the day Poppy sat in Charlton High School.

She had no idea, but people all around the world started copying her. Many didn't succeed. But where there was truth, where there was love, and where there was integrity, people began to be healed. Reports began to come in. Klara van Zyl was the first that day, but not the last.

As Poppy went from her history lesson to maths, a 16-year-old in New Zealand went into the bedroom of her younger sister, who was just 12. The little girl had been battling a brain tumour for six months.

The parents had gone to sleep, but they were both woken by, well, they didn't know what it was. Something must have happened. But then the shouting started down the corridor, and they raced to their daughters and couldn't believe what they found. When they locked eyes with their youngest daughter, they knew something amazing was happening. Something amazingly good.

As Poppy went from her maths lesson to geography, a Canadian woman stood sobbing, as a doctor explained her husband's test results to the shell-shocked couple. They knew something wasn't right, but they had no idea the cancer was so far developed, and the outlook so bad. The woman didn't even wait to get home. They sat together in their car outside the doctor's surgery. Ten minutes later they burst back into the surgery, and the receptionist knew by what she saw in his eyes that she needed to drop everything and get the doctor back here urgently.

As Poppy went from her geography lesson to her lunch break, an Egyptian man finished a packet of macadamia nuts and went to visit his mother.

She was way too young to leave her children and grandchildren behind, he thought, and so he knelt by her bed.

A hot wind was blowing in through the window but he dreamed of her playing with her grandchildren once more.

Power. Shouting. Eyes afire. Healing. Joy.

Poppy sat with her friends at lunch. They always sat together but now none of them sort of knew what to do with Poppy's fame. But mostly they just sat and listened as Poppy explained all of what happened last week. It was truly exciting. But one of them had half an eye on her phone, as the group talked. The girl spoke up, "Poppy I think other people might have started to do it. It says here a woman in South

Africa got better from cancer. And perhaps some other people too."

"What?" said Poppy, "Are you serious?"

"Look" her friend said, as she passed her phone over. Sure enough, it seemed that Elz was the first of many. Poppy was amazed. She didn't know that more miraculous things would happen today. And as she sat there reading social media reports of these healings, it hit her - if she had not told the truth on Friday these people would still have cancer.

Poppy went quiet for a moment. The conversation moved on to something else. Poppy reflected on the news. She started to realise that this was what was meant to happen.

She needed time alone - she needed to process this news. She told the group that she was going to the toilet. As she sat in the cubicle, she mentally worked through the whole journey; all of that anguish on Friday morning, all of the strength to stand up to the lawyer in the courtroom, and to the judge himself.

It was all for this. Joanna had said that it would be OK. She had said that it was the right time for this to be known. Well it was becoming known far more quickly than Poppy had expected. If she had simply told the lies that everyone was expecting on Friday, then she would have been granted bail, there would have been no campaign to release her, the Prime Minister would not have been involved, there would have been no publicity. It would have simply been a mysterious case of possible inside teeking with a trial set down for sometime next year.

But because she told the truth, because she had integrity, a lady in South Africa was walking out of hospital cancer free. It couldn't have happened without Poppy. It couldn't have happened if she didn't tell the truth. As Poppy sat there a smile began to spread across her face. It felt like getting an exam result and finding that you are the top of the class. She had passed the test in the prison cell, and this, not her own freedom, but this news from South Africa, was her reward.

She made her way back to her friends. The smile was still there, and it stayed in place for a long time.

⁓

As the day and the week and the months went on, more and more reports poured in. In every country cancer was losing. Elz, Klara and the others were soon followed by a great number from every nation and every language, a great multitude.

They became known as the teek-healed. For days the internet was filled with their stories, and then their stories became so common that they were no longer newsworthy anymore.

You couldn't buy it. You couldn't fake it. Only where people of strong character were moved by love did it happen.

Chapter Twenty One

Prime Minister King

Six months later, Prime Minister King was in an upbeat mood. His decision to release Poppy Joshua from prison was thoroughly vindicated by the events that had followed. He shuddered to think what would have happened if he hadn't done it. Of course no one gave him credit for his good judgement - in politics they only remember your mistakes. But today he was looking forward to meeting his most famous citizen, which had actually never yet happened.

His driver headed for Charlton. The hospital site Safety Manager had agreed to allow people into the remains of the London Children's Cancer Hospital for this occasion, even though the building was not normally used anymore. So what had once been the foyer of the hospital, was now converted into a venue for the ceremony. The building filled up with press reporters and television crews, as well as a whole bunch of invited guests. Elz was there, with his parents, as the hospital's most famous former patient. Elz wanted to point out to everyone there that he actually got better at school rather than at the hospital, but that might have been a bit too negative. He let it slide.

And Poppy was there of course. Six months as one of the most famous people in world had made her relaxed around cameras. They were part of her life now, regardless of what she wanted. She didn't like it, but she was learning not to care. Her mum was with her, beaming with pride.

Michael, Max, Lloyd and Jake had skipped school for the day and had managed to come along. The four boys were now inseparable. They had just been classmates six months ago. They each had their own interests outside of school. But now they had a bond. They had gone to war together and for the rest of their lives they would regard each other as veterans of a famous battle, one where they had taken on the headmistress, the internet, the Prime Minister and the world.

By winning that battle, they had ended up doing more for the world's sick and suffering than countless thousands of doctors. All before their 15th birthdays. They got past security even though they were not on the official guest list. Their own fame was not that great, but enough to get into a VIP area on the odd occasion. But because of their relationship with Poppy, they got in wherever she was going.

The boys had lost count of the number of times they had simply said, "We're with Poppy", as they breezed past some security guard. These days Poppy had to do a lot of VIP stuff, and the boys never wanted to miss out on the fun.

Prime Minister King entered the room. Every conversation paused and every head turned to see him. Of course his picture was everywhere, but most of the people there had never seen him in the flesh. He greeted various people who were near him, but the whole time he made sure he was moving in Poppy's direction. A few minutes later he shook her hand and greeted her. "So this is the girl from Charlton who's turned the world upside down, is it? A pleasure to meet you Poppy!"

"Thank you Prime Minister. It is a pleasure to meet you too." Poppy smiled broadly and did her best to say hello in a formal enough way, which is surely what you are meant to do when meeting the Prime Minister.

A few minutes later everyone took their seats, and the Prime Minister strode to the podium. He spoke with a clear and strong voice:

"Ladies and gentlemen, for many years the London Children's Cancer Hospital was a place where people from all over this great city received care in the most difficult of times. The service of the staff here was second to none. The building itself was made iconic by the famous *Purple Angels* which covered one whole side of the structure. Six months ago in one remarkable week the Purple Angels were lost to us, and the building was evacuated. Yet, what we gained that week was far greater than what we lost. That week we gained insight into how love can cure cancer. Today, cancer rates are retreating across the planet. Miss Poppy Joshua found a way to utilise the power the macadamia nuts contain to bring health, wholeness and restoration to those whose bodies are suffering. It is the single greatest healthcare breakthrough of our generation. The decline in cancer has meant that there is no need to replace or rebuild this hospital. Other hospitals have absorbed whatever cancer patients remain. This means that London is left with this disused building. So today it gives me great pleasure to announce that the former hospital will be rebuilt as a medical research facility. The mission of healing, of health, and of life that was pursued here for many years will continue. With the research conducted on this site further treatments will be developed to improve the health of the people of this city. Of course they will use more traditional methods than the ones Miss Joshua adopted. But what then of the eastern wall? There have been numerous suggestions put forward. Various artists have proposed *Purple Angels II*, although this time with shatterproof glass."

The room liked the joke, and laughed appreciatively. The Prime Minister continued,

"Other clever and worthwhile ideas have been discussed. However I can further announce today that the eastern wall will be left as it is. The internal doors will be sealed shut and the rooms that faced the wall will of course no longer be used. But by leaving the building this way, we are deliberately making a point about what has happened here."

The crowd were generally thinking that this seemed a bit of an odd idea. It was one that none of them would likely have entertained. But unbeknownst to them, the Prime Minister himself had specifically fought for this idea on the committee that decided what to do with the building. And so the Prime Minster now spoke, and with greater energy, as he made the point clear.

"Every single empty room that faces the street will say to all who pass by, that previously, someone with cancer would be here.

Every empty room says that the cure for cancer that has come into the world is a life-saving miracle.

Every empty room says that we no longer need to care for those dying from cancer because a great many of them are no longer dying.

Every empty room says that the events of the week in which this wall fell, are events that should be memorialised and remembered forever.

Every empty room says that truth, love and integrity are the most important things in the fight against this dreadful disease.

Every empty room says that healing has replaced suffering and the way is opened to all."

The crowd applauded. They had been won over. The building would be a research facility on the inside, and a ruin that makes a point on the outside.

But in the front row Poppy didn't like the idea. She loved it! She was the one who had to commit to the telling the truth when her liberty was in the balance. Everyone else knew about the character that unlocked the power of the macadamia, but she was the one whose character had been tested in a fire that others could only dream about. And she had passed the test. So she loved the Prime Minister's idea.

She loved it so much that in the weeks to come she had a copy of the Prime Minister's speech printed out and put on her bedroom wall. She picked a pretty font and covered the pages with drawings, bright colours and different adornments. But always she had underlined and highlighted those closing words... *the way is opened to all.*

Printed in Great Britain
by Amazon